THE SWEET ROAD BACK

Other Books By Jacki Kelly

THE SWEET ROAD SERIES
The Sweet Road Home
The Sweet Road To Love

DATING JUST GOT SERIOUS
Blind Date
One Date At A Time
Date Me
A Single Date
Speed Date
Dating Just Got Serious – Box Set
Done With Dating

WOMEN'S FICTION
Packed and Ready To Go
Going Backwards

Chapter One

Melissa Conroy-Bellamy needed a few more minutes to pretend she lived another life. The perfect one. The one she began to structure the day she'd graduated from high school, sixteen years ago. Not the one she really lived because she'd fallen in love with the charming man, with the velvet voice rocketing to super-stardom.

From the small window of the plane, she watched as the fog rolled towards the gate along with the aircraft, an appropriate welcome home. The damp, cold San Francisco skyline mirrored the feeling in her gut. But she loved the city. No matter what was going on in the world, the soul of San Francisco always seemed to be happy, even if she wasn't.

The plane taxied to a stop. With a quiet sigh, she grabbed her carry-on bag from under the seat and made her way to the exit. She couldn't pretend anymore. With all the advice she'd offered up to her sisters, it was now time for her to take some of her own words of wisdom.

Every day she chose to ignore the inevitable just prolonged the pain. Her sisters' happy relationships accentuated her misery. Asa and Simeon were expecting their second baby. Dakota and Bishop were off on their honeymoon. How she'd given up on her life, accepting less than the minimum, made her queasy. Believing the promises dripping from Darius's lips as if they were manna from heaven had wrecked her sensibilities.

As she made her way to baggage claim, she fished her cell phone out of her purse, turned it on, and dialed her best friend, Pamela.

"Hey, girl, are you back in town?" Pam asked as soon as she picked up.

"Yep, I just landed. Haven't even picked up my bags yet."

"You don't sound too happy."

"I'm going to do it, Pamela. Either something changes or my marriage is over." She shifted to get out of the way of a man running towards his gate. "I did nothing but think about my future while I was in Bristol. I've had plenty of time to think about my relationship, and I know I don't want to go on this way."

"Well, just don't be hasty. You know Steve and I had one big argument that lasted for months, and I packed my things and left. Not my smartest move. Now, I want him back." Pam had the same lament whenever she talked about Steve.

"No, you don't. You just think you want him because he's dating a tart at the club."

She hesitated. "You're right," she agreed slowly. "But on Saturday night, when I'm sitting home alone, I want him back."

"If Darius doesn't agree to some changes, we can commiserate together on Saturdays. What do you think?" Melissa said as she stepped onto the escalator to baggage claim.

"You might have to fly to Philly if you want to cry on my shoulder. I'm thinking about moving back home. There is nothing keeping me here anymore."

Melissa's throat tightened. Pam was the closest thing she had to a sister on the west coast. The thought of not being able to plop down on Pam's sofa and vent her unhappiness was too depressing to contemplate.

"We need to talk. Let me get my bags, get home, and we can have a real conversation. I want to talk you out of leaving."

"You can try. Bye, Mel." Pam clicked off.

Her red bags circled the luggage carousel. Instead of rushing forward to grab her luggage, she allowed it to cycle again. If Dakota were here, she'd asked her to pull out her sage bundle, light the cloth, and cleanse the aura around San Francisco. She must have picked up some funky stuff because everything was going wrong. Stuck in place, much like everything else, she watched the other passengers collect their bags and hurry off. Rushing to get on with their lives, maybe even excited about the future.

The familiar scent of Darius's cologne greeted her before she saw him. Despite the knot in her stomach, her heart sped up. It always would, no matter what was going on between them. She loved him. That pure, simple fact made her happy and sad.

"I got it." Darius stepped through the crush of people as she reached for her luggage. With one clean jerk, he lifted the heavy bag. He appeared thinner. His True Religion jeans were loose in the legs, but his shirt fit his biceps to perfection. The creamy brown color of his skin was visible from under the familiar baseball cap and dark sunglasses, but his dark, piercing eyes were hidden. The slight upturn of his lips chipped away at the ice surrounding her heart.

"What are you doing here? How did you know when I was arriving?" Melissa stared at her husband. He was more handsome than ever. Her grandmother always said absence made the heart grow fonder. Maybe it worked both ways and he'd be ready for some changes since she'd been away for a few weeks.

He set the bag at her feet and cupped her chin. "I called Asa. She told me." He pressed his lips to hers before she could object. The warm tenderness of his tongue welcomed her home. When he released her, he swiped his thumb against her cheek, the way he used to when they first got married.

The spell was broken when he picked up the satchel and headed toward the exit without saying a word. She had to hurry to keep up with his long strides. From behind, he could have passed for any tall, good-looking man heading into the night. But when he turned around and flashed a smile, his whole face lit up. She understood why women swooned when he sang his love ballads.

She clutched his arm. "Darius, what are you doing? It was nice of you to come down here, but I've got this. I'm sure you must have something else you would rather be doing. Isn't there an appearance or red carpet waiting for you to grace with your presence?"

He glanced over his shoulder but kept walking. In the parking garage, he put her bags in the trunk, unlocked the car, and held the door open for her.

Melissa sat as far from Darius as she could in the small Corvette, wedging her body against the passenger door. As long as she held her anger like a precious stone, her decisions were easier. The man sitting beside her was hard to recognize, very little about him resembled the person she'd married. Sometimes she felt like she was on hold, and if she waited long enough and crossed her fingers really tight, the real Darius, the one she loved, would come back to her.

He backed the car out of the parking space, paid the attendant, and pulled onto the highway. He asked about her trip with genuine curiosity, but she wasn't ready to forgive him for missing her sister's wedding. Whatever was happening in his life always came before her. She'd become his burden instead of his treasure. Her one word replies shut down the conversation. They rode in silence for several miles.

"You never answered my question," Melissa said when he exited the freeway. "Why did you call my sister?"

"Because you wouldn't take my calls. So, I decided to call someone who would. You've been acting like a first-class pain in the ass," he replied without taking his eyes off the road.

"Have you moved your things out of the house like we discussed?"

"No." The edge in his voice matched the sharp tilt of his chin.

"Why not? I thought we agreed. What are you waiting on?"

"Just because you asked me to didn't mean I agreed. I'm not planning on moving any time soon." He pinched her chin and smiled.

His smugness only made her angrier. So used to having his way, he never took anything she said serious enough.

With a huff, Melissa crossed her arms over her chest. "Darius, I don't feel like arguing with you. We talked about this. Our marriage isn't working."

"You said it and, as usual, you expected me to jump. Well, I didn't and I won't. I moved my stuff into the second bedroom, for now. Be happy for the small concession. But I can't promise to stay put. You know the ventilation down there is poor."

"How much longer are we going to dance around this dilemma? I can't keep playing this game of 'when it's convenient for you'. What are the choices this week? Are you married or are you sorting through your options?"

"You know what comes along as part of the business. It has nothing to do with us. We've been over this before. Several artists do the same thing to increase their fan base. It's not forever. Only for right now."

"After five years it has everything to do with us. I'm not living on the edge of your life anymore. , pretending we aren't married to help your career. I'm putting everything into our marriage, and I want you to do the same."

"Melissa, I'm almost there. Dan promised the studio is seriously considering my soundtrack for their movie. Why can't you just play along for a while longer?"

"I've done it for years, and you keep saying just a little longer. I'm not spending this New Year like the past ones. I don't want to live another day hiding behind your stardom. I won't." She paused to swallow the bitter taste collecting in her mouth. "Did you even consider finding another place to live? What about the little house you like in Sausalito?"

He turned left onto Commercial Street without slowing down. "First of all, it's too far from everything. Second, if it's so important for you to move on with your life, then you can move out. You try to find a decent place to live in this neighborhood?" He pulled the car into the porte-cochere and shut off the engine.

"Did you look?"

"No. But I know these things." He applied the emergency brake while staring at her. "Are you coming in?"

The urge to do something different nudged at her, but the cross-country trip had left her bone-tired. Maybe tonight wasn't the time to make any life-altering decisions. They'd managed to put everything off until now, what difference would one more night make?

"Of course, I'm coming in." She cut her eyes and unbuckled her seatbelt. Without waiting for him, she marched up the concrete stairs of their Victorian-style home. Inside, the familiar smell of lavender that should have greeted her, did not. The ornate crystal tray with the shredded potpourri wasn't working.

There should have been something comforting about being home. Mim, her grandmother, had a million sayings, one for every occasion. Her favorite one, there was no place like home, should have applied as Melissa set her purse on the entry table, but she couldn't muster the sentiment.

"Why do you have every light turned on? I feel like I'm in Times Square." Melissa walked up the four stairs leading to the living area.

"I left in a hurry," Darius said. "I had to track you down, remember."

She made her way to the kitchen. For a moment, she couldn't focus on any one thing because so much drew her attention. The neat freak in her suppressed a scream. The moment her gaze landed on the teetering stack of dishes in the sink, the stuffed trashcan grabbed her attention. Her usually pristine kitchen looked like a category-five hurricane had blown through it. Every inch of counter space was covered with half-filled glasses with varying hues of liquids. A box of cereal, two empty beer cans, and three cans of berry-flavored energy drinks cluttered the table. Two 12-pack cartons of the same drink were stacked next to the refrigerator. The aroma of soiled dishes assaulted her nose.

"Darius, what the…?" She spun around to face him.

"I've been busy. I've almost finished the last tracks, so I didn't have time to clean."

"Why didn't you let Margie take care of it? That's what we pay her for."

"She had some family emergency and hasn't been here for two weeks. But you wouldn't know about her troubles since every time your sisters call, you jump on a plane and head off to Delaware. Do you ever think about what I might need? If you were here taking care of our home, I might have finished my tracks by now."

"Dakota was getting married. What should I have done, blown her off to sit home and wait for you to show up and play happy homemaker?" She tried to contain the anger bubbling in her stomach. "It's my family. I miss them. When I'm there, I'm not required to stand in the background pretending I'm just an admiring groupie."

"Here we go again." He rolled his eyes toward the ceiling and reached in the refrigerator for an energy drink. "I do this because Dan is sure I'll attract more attention from fans if people think I'm single." He opened the can and downed the contents.

"I don't want to hear what Dan wants anymore. If it's more important for you to have fans than to have a wife, I'll grant your wish."

"I'll get the kitchen in the morning," he commented as he set the empty can on the counter with all the other clutter.

She hadn't expected a response about giving him his wish. But some facial expression or sign of regret for the state of their marriage would have been nice. She sniffed the air, and then covered her nose. "What is that smell? It's disgusting."

"Oh, yeah. I got a puppy." A small, blue crate was pushed into the corner of the room. Through the mesh across the door, she spotted two huge brown eyes.

Darius opened the door, and a blond dog with paws the size of a bear bounded across the floor. Happy to be free, he circled the island with his tail wagging so fast his hindquarters seemed to shake.

"Are you kidding me? Who is going to take care of a puppy?"

"A fan left him for me backstage last week. What was I supposed to do with him?"

"Give him to Dan. Doesn't he handle all your problems?"

"I tried. He wouldn't take the little fellow."

With a whimper, the puppy blinked up at her, tilted his head, and then squatted in front of her to relieve his bladder on the tip of her camel suede Manolo Blahnik bootie.

"Ahhh," she screamed and jumped backed, crashing into the plates on the counter while trying to reach a paper towel. "Tell me this did not just happen. Tell me this is a bad dream sequence. Do you know what these shoes cost? I've only worn them once. Darius…I—"

"Calm down, Melissa. I'm sure a little pee won't stain." He snatched the paper from her hand and dabbed her right foot. "See, you can barely see anything."

"I can see it just fine." She glared at him. "Who is going to clean up this mess and get rid of the odor permeating our home? You were supposed to be moving out. Instead, you find a stray to move in and he's not trained. Come on, Darius. Does Dan think it's okay for you to be a pet owner?" She stomped her foot.

He scooped up the dog and pushed him out the back door into the fenced yard. "It's just a dog. He's trained. You must have made him nervous." Darius flashed a smile that used to melt her heart a few years ago, but tonight, she refused to allow his charm to penetrate her carefully constructed barrier. Giving in to him only worked to her disadvantage. His big, bright smile short-circuited her ability to think. She stiffened her backbone. Before she would have forgiven him for his infamous transgressions.

But not now. Her weakness had set them on their current path.

"Does the rest of the house look like a dumping zone?"

Instead of answering her, he bit his bottom lip, which only meant he was getting ready to lose his temper.

She exhaled and kept her hands planted on her hips to keep from flying about the room like a witch on steroids. "Darius, I'm exhausted. I've spent the better part of the day going through security, dealing with a flight delay, having a baby scream in my ears, and now dog pee. I'm going to bed. Is it too much to ask when I come downstairs in the morning the house be ready for human inhabitants and the stench gone?"

"I've got to get back to the studio." He opened the door and allowed the dog to trot back in. After securing him in the crate, he turned out the light. "I can't make any promises. But I'm glad you're home."

"Darius, don't you dare leave this house without taking this with you." She opened the crate and reached for the dog. After placing him in Darius' arms, she marched upstairs.

****

Darius wanted a kiss. The whole time she was gone, he'd imagined her homecoming. He'd grab her by her narrow waist, lift her lithe frame into the air, and taste her luscious lips. It's the only thing his brain could hold on to. But her posture in the airport had warned him off like blaring red lights. Get too close and her automatic dart throwers would activate.

She'd stormed upstairs, her sandy-colored ponytail bouncing with each step. The ringlets falling across her face had made it difficult to see her eyes.

"Yep, you always meet my expectations too," he yelled. Her tight, designer wool slacks disappeared into the master bedroom, followed by a loud slamming of the door.

He suppressed a chuckle before placing the dog back in the crate. He grabbed his keys and locked the door behind him.

"Well, that didn't go too well," he said, before sliding into the driver seat. But playing by Melissa's rules was history. No matter what he did, she was unhappy, so the hell with trying. Judging by the scowl on her face since leaving the airport, nothing much had changed. She was hell-bent on flushing their marriage down the toilet. And he damn well felt like letting her. Years of watching his father trying to please his mother proved only one thing. Some women couldn't be satisfied. But unlike his father, he wouldn't spend years trying.

He backed onto the street and yanked the gearshift into drive. Melissa's only intention was to see how miserable she could make him. And in the two hours they'd spent together tonight, she was as good at it as ever.

Once the soundtrack for his new music was finished, he'd have more time. Pushing back the release date to deal with Melissa wasn't an option. Music had occupied his life since his parents had given him his first bass guitar at thirteen. That had been the best Christmas until the first one he'd spent with Melissa.

Sitting at a red light, the memory of the two of them sitting on the floor and opening those first gifts made him smile. She had given him the perfect one. The antique record player he'd admired for years still sat on the entertainment center in their living room. He hadn't used it in months, but he still treasured the gift. The traffic light changed and he accelerated through the intersection.

His father was his biggest fan. Snagging the movie contract would make his dad even more proud. A few dirty dishes was no big deal. Melissa thought life should be perfect, but he knew better. Watching his parents hold their marriage together after his mother's infidelity taught him the sacrifices life demanded from a soul. Somehow, his father forgave her and their marriage limped along.

Forgiveness was a funny thing. Melissa claimed to forgive him. But whenever she got the chance to snip at him, she did. Two years was a long time to pay for one mistake. Strolling into the Grammy Awards without her was stupid. He had to trust Dan's opinion. Dan knew the music business and what was the use of paying him fifteen percent if he wasn't going to take his advice.

Deep down inside, Melissa probably had no intentions of ever moving beyond their bad times. She dreamed up ways to dig her five-inch heels into his heart. Either she had to move beyond the awards incident or he would have to move on. Long suffering wasn't a role he wanted to play. His father was doing it well enough for the both of them.

Darius massaged his earlobe. Just thinking about how much he'd hurt her made him flinch. He was uncertain which felt worse, her wrath for the past two years or the guilt chewing at him? If their marriage stood any chance of surviving, they needed to find a way to leave the past where it belonged. It sounded about as impossible as getting her to like the new puppy.

Chapter Two

Melissa hugged the pillow to her chest without opening her eyes. Climbing out of bed meant going to do battle with the troubles in her life. And she wasn't ready to fight with Darius. Coffee. A huge mug of black joe might help her tackle her day, but her life needed a lot more.

She flopped onto her side. Just outside the window a thick gray cloud drifted in front of the sun. Today promised to be just as gloomy as the day before. The house was quiet, which meant either Darius hadn't come back home last night or he was still asleep. Falling in love with Darius had been easy. He had been the most popular guy in their graduating class. Every woman in her sorority house had wanted to date the starting quarterback who was known to break into an impromptu song. While Melissa tutored him to ensure he passed his final exams, Darius had emitted a charm as noxious as carbon monoxide, and somewhere between quadratic equations and experimental philosophy, he'd planted a kiss on her that remained in her memory all these years later.

By the time he told her he was moving to California to become the hottest singer since Prince, she was so in love she would have followed him naked down Main Street. She squeezed her eyes shut to block the recollection. Burying her dreams to help him sounded good back then. But he never seemed to appreciate or recognize the sacrifice.

She pushed the pillow away and climbed out of bed. Five-year-old memories weren't worth holding on to. With a Grammy and several records on the Billboard chart, he was supposed to be content and ready to spend more time on their relationship. Instead, he'd managed several cheating rumors, leaving her stranded at an awards ceremony, and endless invitations to the best parties around the country. The tabloid reports claiming he'd screwed his backup singer two years ago still made her cringe.

Beside the bed she found her pink slippers and pushed her feet into them. After washing up, she made her way downstairs to the kitchen. The only way to think through her life was with something on her stomach.

At the bottom of the stairs, she drew a deep breath. The same awful smell greeted her again this morning. She peeked around the corner, hoping to see her immaculate state-of-the-art kitchen back to normal.

"What are you doing here?" she asked.

Darius spun around. His shirtless chest was front page ready. Each defined pectoral muscle caught her attention. For a brief moment, she allowed her eyes to linger on his fine physique before swallowing the saliva collecting in her mouth.

"I live here," he responded and turned back to the television. His ripped back was as gorgeous as the front. She tried to ignore the horny elf sitting on her shoulder, reminding her she hadn't had sex in weeks.

The shamble from last night looked more disgusting in the bright light of day. The mess drained her, making her feel unsteady. She gripped the edge of the chair for balance, or was it comfort?

He pulled a clean cup from the dishwasher, while his new faithful friend was sprawled across the entrance, licking his paw.

"Coffee?" Darius asked.

"What happened? I thought you were going to take care of this mess?" She inched towards the counter, careful not to upset the stack of dishes threatening to tumble, or get too close to Darius. Keeping a distance between them was good. And even better if she didn't have to peer at his perfect body.

"I never said any such thing." He poured coffee into a mug with her name scripted across the front. "Here you go. Just the way you like it."

The dog trotted over to her.

"Keep your attack animal away from me. If he pisses on my house shoes, I'm going to hit you with them."

"Calm down. I just had him outside. He's fine. I think he likes you," Darius said without looking at her.

"There is no use in him liking me. The three of us won't be together long enough for it to be worth his while." She sipped the coffee and nestled her butt onto the bar stool, making an effort to focus on something in the backyard. Anything to take her mind off the magnet pulling her toward Darius; even a field of dandelions would do.

Darius came around the counter and sat next to her. "Why not? Don't you know a dog is man's best friend?"

"Why don't you go put some clothes on?"

He glanced down at his flat stomach and flexed his abdominal muscles. "I thought you liked my abs."

"Used to. Not anymore. Pretty boys are a dime a dozen."

He ran his hand along her back. She tried not to ease into his touch, but her body relaxed against her will.

"We don't have to be mean to each other, do we?" he asked.

"No. You're right. We need to make some decisions. It's a new year and there's no time like the present." She put her cup down and lifted his hand off her back. She couldn't concentrate while he touched her.

"You sound like you've given this a lot of thought."

"Unlike you, I have. I can't seem to stop thinking about us and what's happening to our marriage. I tried to forget all the headlines, the Facebook posts, and the media gossip. I want to believe you when you tell me you've been faithful. But this isn't the life for me. Spending so much time alone, always wondering." She stared at the dark brew in her cup, while she tried to form the right words. "Do you remember when I told you about my parents? How a few months before they died, there was a rumor my father was having an affair and maybe fathered another child?"

She held the handle of the cup while keeping her head down. "I have no idea what my mother was feeling. She never let on. But I made a promise to myself back then. I never wanted to live under a cloud. Maybe I'm not as strong as my mother or maybe I'm tougher than she was." She rushed on before the familiar lump of sorrow formed in her throat, stopping her from telling her truth. "Either way, the last year has been unbearable for me. I don't plan to spend another year the same way."

"Well, it seems like you have this covered." He pushed off the stool and left his cup as he walked out.

****

Darius drew a deep breath as he climbed the stairs. Damned if he would just sit there while she ripped his heart out. He wasn't some hick she'd picked out of a cornfield. Women threw their panties at him, sometimes without taking them off first.

"Darius, you forgot your dog," she yelled to him.

"Come on, boy. Come on," he called for the puppy.

"Don't you want to talk about this?"

He turned to see her posed at the foot of the stairs. The dog took the steps one at a time like a nervous toddler. "Can't, I've got an appointment. We'll have to catch up later. Besides, you've got it pretty well figured out. So, let's just go with your plan."

"You always expect me to fix stuff, don't you? Well, this time, maybe the both of us need to work on it together."

"You see, there's where you're wrong. I'm willing to let you be you, without giving direction all the time." He locked eyes with her for several seconds, refusing to let her divert his attention.

After several moments, she blinked and focused on the dog. "What's the dog's name? He has to have a name."

"Yeah, I'll get around to naming him soon." He picked up the struggling animal and carried him to the bedroom. With the door closed, he dressed in jeans, a button-down shirt, and a blazer. Sooner or later, he'd have to sit down and talk to Melissa, but only when he had some answers. Maybe when her anger subsided a bit. Getting dumped was new for him. But Melissa was supposed to have his back, support him. Instead, she wanted to bail.

He picked up his cell phone and dialed his agent. "Dan, I'm tired of waiting. I need to get this mess straightened out. Now."

"Darius, my man." Dan sounded happy, but the familiar snap of a lid indicated he was fumbling for an antacid. "You know I'm working on things for you. It takes a little time. Your new album will be better than your last. The promo leading up to the release has been fantastic, hasn't it?"

"It's great. I hardly have enough time to finish the last two cuts because you've got me running all over the country to every party you think the paparazzi will show up to." He ran his hand over his close-cropped cut. "This is getting a little unbearable."

"It's good publicity. And right now you can use every headline you can get. I've been getting calls from LA. They're interested. Stay close to your phone; I might have something later today."

"Dan, this is my life—"

"I'm taking good care of you. You just keep making the music and I'll keep selling those hits."

"What about the tabloid article? Did you get it straightened out?"

"Tell Melissa to ignore them. We can't waste money trying to fight trash. As soon as we quash one, another one will spring up to replace it."

"I know the drill." Darius disconnected the call.

Getting out of the house without running into Melissa was about as likely as her planting warm, passionate kisses on him. As he came down the stairs, he spotted her seated in the kitchen, swinging her pink-slippered foot at a maddening speed.

"I'm going to the studio," he said, after securing the dog.

"Sure you are. You've just found a new hiding place, haven't you?"

He picked up his keys and headed for the door.

She jumped up. "I'm catching a ride. After you're done, we can stop by Saks. You owe me a pair of shoes." She dashed out before he could respond.

It was forty-five minutes before she came back.

"I was hoping to get there sometime this afternoon." He made a grand gesture of looking at his watch.

"Everything is all about you, isn't it?" She picked up her purse and walked out ahead of him. Her seductive hips only highlighted the point he hadn't touched them in weeks.

Once they were on I-80, he turned on the radio. Some song about booty blared.

"I'm not listening to musical nonsense." Melissa reached for the dial.

"My car, my radio." He placed his hand on top of hers and lifted it away. It wasn't the station he wanted, but since she'd made him wait so long, it was the only way to strike back, for now.

He pulled into a parking garage near Market Street and turned off the car. "So, what are you going to do while I'm recording?"

"Oh no. I'm going in with you." She opened the car door and climbed out.

"This could take a little time. Hours." He walked a few steps ahead of her.

"I don't have a thing to do. You owe me a pair of $600 shoes and I plan to collect them. Today."

"We don't have to do this now, do we? You know I'm good for the money," he offered.

"We could wait a few days until you forget, right?"

Every day, Melissa found a new way to dig at him. If she was as unhappy as she seemed, maybe she was right. Letting her go would be the right thing to do. His father still held on to his mother, but she always seemed to be somewhere else. No matter how hard he tried.

He held the building door open for Melissa. The studio was on the second floor of a small nondescript building. Dan had found it, and even though the rent was sky high, the soundproofing made it worthwhile.

"You can wait out here or come in the back. Your choice." He pointed to the small leather sofa but kept walking to the equipment room. After powering up the instruments, he sat in the large cushioned chair and placed the headphones over his ears.

He fired up the tracks from the night before and listened as his voice cooed back at him. With his eyes closed, he tried to detect why the sound didn't stir him. It was a love ballad with no emotion.

After the second run, he adjusted the bass and let it run again. Midway through the song, the door opened. Melissa walked in and took the seat next to him.

"Let me hear it," she said.

"Are you sure you want to listen? The song's not finished yet."

"I want to see what's got your brow wrinkled."

The song continued to play through the headphones for a few moments before he backed it up and turned the speakers on. The short musical intro played before his voice eased into the song.

I know you're slippin away.
Can't hardly face the day
Shouldn't have to live this way
Stay by my side. Stay by my side…my
side…side

She tapped her short, red fingernails against the metal on the chair in tune with the music. Her eyes closed and she seemed to drift away on the melody. Neither said a word until the song ended.

"What do you think?"

Melissa nodded. "It's good."

"Good? Is that the best you can say about the song?"

"Your last album was better. Is this supposed to be the lead song?"

"Yes."

"You're not singing like you mean the words or feel them. You might as well be singing this in the shower while you're lathering your armpits." She pushed her chair back and stood up.

"I've recorded this three times. I've had the whole crew working on this track."

"What can I say? I'm not feeling your emotion in the music."

He powered down the machine and stood. "I've got two weeks to get this straight. If I don't, then I might as well forget my chance of convincing the studio they want the music. It's over."

"You'll get it right. You always do. Everything you touch turns to gold." She smiled. The gesture melted away all the harsh words from earlier.

The shrill ring of his cell phone erupted in the room. Hearing the special tone set for Dan made his flesh pebble.

"It's Dan. I need to get this." He picked up the phone.

"Of course you do. God forbid the Great Dan Schumacher should have to wait."

He turned his back. "What's up?"

"Glad I caught you. Put on your A-list gear. You're going to the Mansion party tonight. It's rumored anyone who's anyone will be there."

"Ah…ah. I guess I can make it. At least you're earning your money. What time is the car picking us up?"

"You're killing me here, Darius." Dan's exaggerated moan vibrated in Darius's ear. "There is no us. Not yet. The car will pick you up in three hours. You and only you. Just make sure you look hot and available." He hung up.

Darius slid the phone in his pocket.

Melissa pulled on her leather jacket. "Come on, Saks awaits."

His tongue knotted. The constant tug between Dan and Melissa rankled him. They seemed bent on polarizing wants. The moment Dan requested him here; she demanded his attention there. Their stipulations dulled the shiny aura surrounding his music. Life was a lot less complicated when he'd sat behind the desk of the family company and raked in the money.

The ideal thing would have been to take Melissa's hand and fly her back to Bristol, where life was plain and simple and their love wasn't challenged ninety times a day. But he'd made a promise to his father and he planned to keep his commitment. He'd never let his father down before. And even the stink-eye Melissa gave him wouldn't make him start now.

"Melissa, I can't. Not tonight. I've got an appearance to make."

Her face clouded, and for one brief moment, he thought she was going to cry. Seeing her unhappy made his chest tighten. She spun towards the door. "Before my shoes?"

"I'm afraid so. We'll have to go shopping for them another day. Maybe tomorrow." He wanted his tone to soften her disappointment. But hoping she'd see he would rather be with her than hanging out for publicity was like trying to fill a bucket of water with a thimble.

"Sure, Darius." Icicles dripped from her voice. "I've got a million of your promises just waiting to be fulfilled.

Chapter Three

The limousine slowed in front of the private club. From the darkened interior of the car, Darius saw women who all looked the same, standing in line to get inside. Pretty women all eager and excited to dance, or drink, or meet one of the new and upcoming musicians. From the other side of the street, camera bulbs flashed like twinkling lights.

With a deep breath, he stepped out and flashed the megawatt smile he had perfected for his fans. Hearing the roar of his name never got old. A shot of adrenaline raced through him like a strike of lightening, giving him the juice he needed to get through the night.

"You're late," Dan said as they walked into the dark club. Without waiting for a reply, Dan shoved a pen in his hand.

"I think you forget I have a life. One I used to really enjoy. I thought I was going to spend an evening with my wife before you interrupted my plans. I also have a release I'm trying to finish in two weeks." Darius signed the palm of a young woman who looked like she should be at home finishing her homework.

"You can complain when you have the contract for the movie deal."

Darius scribbled his initials on papers and cocktail napkins shoved in front of him as they made their way to the second tier. Before taking a seat in the circular leather booth, a server popped the cork on a bottle of champagne and handed him a glass.

"I hope Melissa understands about tonight." Dan surveyed the room. "As you can see, tonight all eyes are on you. If she had showed up, then everyone would be focusing on that young rapper who still needs his mama to wipe his nose." Dan used his chin to point across the room where an entourage of young men sat in a similar booth and surveyed the dance floor below.

Darius gulped the sparkling wine and refilled the glass before replying. "She's made it quite clear she won't play my girlfriend any longer. She wants all or nothing, and the way I've been pushing her lately, she's closer to taking the nothing route."

"Talk to her so she'll understand how small of a sacrifice this isto make for your passion. We need to make sure you stay relevant. Having your name and pictures in social media or on the print pages just means more dollars in the bank."

"We talk plenty and thank you for staying out of my personal life. I don't need your help with my marriage."

Dan grinned, flashing his chemically whitened teeth. "Yeah, okay. Anyway, about getting you in the papers…" He tapped the base of his glass. "Are you having an affair I can leak to the press, or how about a DUI?"

Darius turned away. The same conversation came up every time they got together. The only thing Dan found interesting was how much money he could put in his account.

From across the room, a petite woman with warm brown coloring and long, platinum-blonde hair winked at him. She ran her tongue over her glossy lips without breaking eye contact. She could have been a cover model, a stripper, or even a lioness, from the distance it was hard to tell.

Darius returned his attention to Dan. "What's the plan for this evening? I'm not staying long."

"You just got here; you can't leave yet. I'm expecting some studio brass to show up later this evening. Smile at the ladies, make them feel special. You know the routine."

"Do I need to be here for such a trivial discussion? Isn't that why I pay you a commission?" He drained his glass.

"They like to see what they're buying." Dan grinned.

"I didn't know we were selling me."

Without commenting, Dan slid out of the booth and disappeared in the crowd. Darius examined the room. At thirty-three, he had to be one of the oldest men in the club. This should have been fun, but without Melissa seated beside him, it was about as fun as a blizzard in July.

A yawn gathered in the back of his throat. As he worked to suppress it, the leggy feline with the unnatural hair color slinked across the room and dropped into the seat next to him.

"We're not keeping you awake, are we?" She pursed her lips and reached for his champagne. After swallowing the contents, leaving her lipstick imprinted on the crystal, she set the glass down in front of him with a thump.

"No. It's just been a long night. I'm working a lot of hours, so I'm a little drained." He eased the wine flute away from him to the middle of the table.

"Yes, I know. I can't wait for your new album to come out. My name is Bambi, by the way." She purred like a kitten and leaned closer to him. Her dewy, smooth cleavage nearly spilled out of her top. The intoxicating sexuality she transmitted was nauseating. She was trying too hard. By the time she reached thirty, she'd have nothing left.

"You're kidding me, right? Were you named after a strip star or are you getting on the pole tonight?" He looked over her head for Dan. Whether Dan came back or not, in less than five minutes, he planned to leave.

Bambi slid closer and placed her hand on top of his while her other hand slid to his crotch.

While pressing her breasts against his arm, flash bulbs popped, blinding him for several seconds.

"Shit." He drew away from Bambi.

Bambi slid out of the booth and was half-way across the room before he fished some bills out of his wallet and dropped them on the table. Several patrons had turned their attention to the commotion and were taking pictures with their cell phones. Heat started at the base of his spine and migrated up his back, igniting every hair on his body before settling around his neck. He released the button on his collar and glared around the packed club.

"Hey, where are you going?" Dan rushed him.

"You set me up, didn't you?"

"What? It's just a few pictures."

He grabbed Dan by the sleeve of his expensive jacket. "I told you I'm not doing this kind of childish shit anymore. You're fucking with my marriage, and I won't allow anyone to mess within my personal business. Either get with the program or I'll find someone who will." Flashbulbs continued to pop.

"Calm down, Darius. I did it for you," Dan said, before sitting. "Besides, we've got a contract. Ironclad."

Darius stood five inches taller than Dan. He stepped around the table and bent so close to Dan, he could see the pores around his nose. With his finger pointed, he said, "I don't give a rat's ass about a contract. I've broken bad ones before and I'll do it again. You don't want to mess with me, Dan," he said through clenched teeth. "I might be new to the music industry, but don't think I'm a chump. It won't end pretty. You can bank on my words."

****

Melissa switched off the television and stared at the black screen. If her sisters could see her now, they'd shake their heads in disbelief. The fierce-talking, get-to-the-point Melissa was mired in mud and couldn't fight her way out. Giving direct advice was a lot easier than taking it.

She swung her legs off the couch and padded into the kitchen. The clock on the microwave read 11:00 p.m. Too early to go to bed and too late to go out for dinner. She surveyed the mess, which only seemed to get worse. Cooking was out of the question; there wasn't a clean dish left in the cabinet. After calling her favorite pizza joint, she dialed Pam's cell phone number.

"Tell me you're out having a good time," she said to her best friend.

"I wish. I've got my pajamas on and I'm reading a book. Ain't that a helluva way to spend Saturday night?"

"I was watching a dating reality show. I think we're tied for pathetic."

36

"Where's Darius?"

"He went to some event. Again, I wasn't invited. I should start a club for abandoned wives of famous people." The silly joke only made her feel worse.

"Sorry about your situation, sweetie."

"Don't worry about me. I won't be doing this much longer. Anyway, what's this about you moving to Philly? Are you going to leave me, too?"

"I'll leave my heart in San Francisco, but I'm taking my butt to the east coast. I need a change. Maybe I'll pull myself out of this blue funk when I'm away from all the memories Steve and I made together here. At least I can hope a change of scenery will help."

The doorbell rang. "My pizza is here. I better go. When you move, get a place big enough for me to have a room. I might be joining you pretty soon."

"Not if you know what I know. Find a way to make it work. Darius has a good heart and you still love him."

"We'll talk." Melissa disconnected the call and fished twenty dollars from her purse to pay for her meal. When she settled at the kitchen island and opened the box, the rich aroma of melted cheese and Canadian bacon filled her nostrils as she pulled out a slice.

Before she could take a bite, the dog began scratching at his crate.

"Did the smell wake you up?" She slid off the stool and glared into the dog's big, brown eyes. "Why don't you come out?" She released the latch. He ran out and licked her cheek.

"We aren't friends, but you can keep me company tonight. Just don't think about peeing in the house."

She returned to her seat and sniffed the slice of pizza before taking a bite. The hot cheese felt good in her mouth, but it tasted bland. She took another bite. This was her favorite indulgence and her favorite toppings. It should have tasted better and made her happy. Her shoulders slumped as she closed the lid on the box.

"Since I can't eat my dinner, I might as well drink my dinner. What do you think?" she asked the dog, before pulling a bottle of Merlot from the wine refrigerator and popping the cork.

She rolled the wine glass between her palms. Maybe drinking could fill all the empty hours stretching in front of her. Mim would say, 'you can't find happiness in the bottom of a bottle'. But Mim didn't know everything. She couldn't, she only graduated from high school. Melissa had her beat by six additional years of college and grad school. Plus, Mim never had such good wine. The

closest Mim came to libations was a hot toddy to
fend off a cold.

Melissa's intention was not to wait up for
Darius. But the more she drank, the more the anger
piled on. It had nothing to do with the shoes. His
attitude sucked. Stardom must have crowded out his
common sense, or maybe he didn't want a small-
town girl anymore. His universe catered to him.
Like a fading star, she no longer held the coveted
position as his prize anymore.

She pulled a tissue from the pocket of the
robe and dabbed the tears. She shoved it back with a
promise. Enough feeling sorry for herself, it was
time to do something different.

The slamming front door jarred her back to
reality. The dog scrambled to his feet, ran to the
entrance, and started to bark. From her position in
the kitchen, she heard Darius greet the puppy. The
dog's claws clicked on the tiled kitchen floor as he
strolled back released a rousing yawn, and then sat
at her feet.

"Some watch-dog you're going to make. I
don't think there's much need for barking after the
person is in the house," she said.

Darius was home early. The action in the
club must not have met his expectations or he'd still
be there cheesing for the cameras.

Darius entered the kitchen and stopped. His
eyes registered surprise when they landed on her. In

his black leather blazer, gray houndstooth vest and white shirt, he was mouth-watering gorgeous. "What are you doing up?"

"Since when have I had to report to you?" She took another sip and held the liquid in her mouth several moments before swallowing. Now, she sounded bitter. She set the glass down and shook her head to change her attitude. "I couldn't sleep."

"How much have you had to drink?" He placed her wine glass in the kitchen sink. "What's going on?"

She reached around him for the glass and swallowed the last of the wine. "What are you now, my father?"

He flopped into the chair.

"Why are you home so early? Wasn't the club exciting?" she asked.

"I don't feel like fighting with you tonight." She detected exhaustion in his voice.

"Then there is something we both agree on." She took the chair opposite him. "So, you didn't answer me. Why are you back so early?"

"Dan pulled another one of his stunts." He opened a bottle of energy drink and took a swallow.

"What was it this time? Did he prop you behind a table to sign autographs all night?" She giggled. Maybe he was right about her being drunk.

He ran his palm over his face. "There may be pictures tomorrow or pictures in the next addition of the gossip rags."

One of her fluffy slippers tumbled from her foot and dropped to the floor. There wasn't much fuzz left on the tip. Time to buy new ones. Her relationship with her shoes was better than the relationship with her husband. The thought should have made her sad, instead, it only numbed the anger rolling in her stomach since he'd dropped her off like a sack of laundry.

"Okay, Darius. I know I'm going to be sorry I asked this question, but what pictures?" She drew a deep breath, hoping he'd say something that wouldn't cut her right down the middle.

He sighed. "In the club, Dan set it up. Some stripper chick and me."

"And what were the two of you doing? Kissing, making out?"

"Neither. And I'll handle it." His chair scraped against the floor as he stood.

She squeezed her eyes tight to block out the vision. His nonchalance was as abrasive as what might greet her on the front page of the paper. Where did you get the backbone to ignore your husband kissing someone else?

Instead of letting him walk away, anger pushed her to pick a fight with him. Tonight, he couldn't stroll in, drop ugly news on her, and then saunter away as if it meant nothing.

"And what do you suggest I do in the meantime, hide out in the basement? Pretend it never happened? Should I look the other way, hoping anyone who knows me doesn't see those photos? You've made me a laughing stock again."

"I said I'll handle it, Melissa, and I will."

"You said the same thing when he pushed me aside last year at the awards ceremony so you'd get photographed alone. And the time before that when you were convinced showing up at the festival with me on your arm wasn't a good idea."

"I get it, Melissa. Do you think I don't know what's going on here?" His voice was tight, like he was trying to control his emotions.

She couldn't stop now. Mim always preached 'if you can't say something nice, don't say anything'. But tonight, he needed to see her pain. No more pretending she could handle this life. "I don't think you do. If you did, Dan would be gone by now."

His eyes narrowed, riveting her to the stool. "I said I can take care of it and I will. I'm going to bed." He peeled off his jacket and walked out of the room.

Moments later, the sound of his record player drifted into the kitchen. Listening to oldies meant he was trying to unwind. The old Jeffrey

Osborne love song mellowed her mood too. Even though she didn't want to, her body swayed to the melody.

Chapter Four

Melissa woke up feeling sluggish. She extracted the handheld mirror from the nightstand drawer to stare at the puffy, dark circles under her eyes. The ugly truth stared back at her. She pressed the pad of her index finger against the thin skin. Today would require a heavy slathering of cover-up. Just another indicator she wasn't doing a good job of managing her situation.

She wanted to claim her life, her emotions, her marriage, so she could feel normal again. It was time to break free from the cocoon restricting her.

Darius was happy to be married to his music sheets and the hundreds of drooling female fans who multiplied every night. She brushed the soggy tissues from the bed into the wicker wastebasket before pulling the sheet and comforter up to her chin.

No matter what her heart wanted, she refused to live this sham another day. Tossing and turning every night couldn't be good for her and did nothing to improve her emotional state either. But the finality of ending their marriage was too painful. There weren't any words from Mim to comfort her through this.

She threw back the covering and crawled out of bed. Today was just as good as any to make a change. Getting in the shower, she adjusted the water temperature to cool the shock of the hot spray.

The perfect dress to see a lawyer would never be found on the cover of Vogue or Lucky magazine, so the royal blue, simple sheath was as good as any. She slipped on her favorite pair of black pumps and made her way downstairs without taking the time to put on makeup or even checking her reflection in the mirror. It was enough to be fully dressed.

Darius had left the house at eight, just as the temperature began to creep up. From the bedroom, she'd heard him talking on the phone and playing with his puppy. Since their run-in two weeks ago, they had exchanged a total of twenty words. She'd kept count.

The kitchen remained the same. At least something in the house was consistent. Even the smell was the same. Instead of eating at home, anything from the corner deli sounded better.

She released the dog from his cage and rubbed his chin. He placed his paw on her shoe. The warmth from his soulful eyes calmed her. But getting attached to him would only make leaving San Francisco harder. She scratched his head. "At least you like me, don't you?"

She picked up the phone and dialed Asa's number. Talking to her sister was like taking a Valium.

"Hey, Melissa," Asa responded to her greeting.

"Do you remember how Mom used to tell us to partner well, our lives depended on it? The three of us would roll our eyes every time she recited that mantra. But now I get it. I had no idea the man I married would impact my health, my wealth, my lineage, or my location. Just thinking about it all is so exhausting." She didn't realize she was holding her breath until she panted.

"I remember. But what made you dig up that old saying now?"

"I can't stop thinking about it. Partner well. Simple words packed with so much meaning." Melissa tugged her hair around her finger while she stared out the window above the sink, focusing on nothing.

"How's it going? Any better?" Asa asked.

"No. If the atmosphere in this house gets any colder, we'll be competing with the Arctic."

"Who's winning the kitchen cold war?"

"Darius. I've decided to use paper plates and eat take-out food. I've put on five pounds since getting home. I only want comfort food, which means pasta and hamburgers."

"Well, at least you're eating. The last time I saw you, you could have used a few pounds."

"Yeah, well, you should see me now. As for the kitchen, pretty soon I'm expecting to see something crawling across the kitchen counter. Enough about me. How's the pregnancy, and what does Mia have to say about the baby?"

"She's excited. Every day she wants to know if this is the day the baby will come. Maybe Simeon and I should have waited until the ninth month and ninth day to tell her about having a baby brother."

In the beginning, she and Darius had talked about having children. The idea of her being a mother one day used to make her silly with happiness. Now, the thought she'd never have children with Darius twisted her stomach into a tight knot.

"Are you showing yet?" Melissa asked, pushing away the pain.

"I've been showing since I was three months. I feel like a balloon getting noticeably bigger every day. But, Melissa, I'm worried about you. What are you going to do? You and Darius can't live with this much hostility for long."

"As a matter of fact, I'm on my way to see a lawyer today. I'm filing for divorce."

Her sister gasped. "Are you sure? Don't you want to try counseling first?"

"We don't have a problem with our marriage, Asa. Darius is already married. He's in love with his music. I'm the other woman."

"Are you going alone? Seeing a lawyer isn't something you should do all by yourself." If Asa was in the room with her, Melissa imagined her sister would wrap her in a maternal hug and rock her.

"I'm a big girl. I'll be fine. I think I'd rather do this by myself. I thought about asking Pam, but she's pretty fragile right now. I'll meet her later for dinner. Her husband ran out on her a few months back, so she'll understand my mood."

"Did you find a good lawyer? Since Darius is a trust-fund-baby, his family had his finances straightened out before he started walking. This might turn ugly."

"There's a billboard near the school with a picture of a lawyer with a beard. I'm going to give him a try."

"Is he any good?"

Melissa shrugged her shoulder. "I don't want anything from Darius, so it doesn't matter."

"Does he know?"

"He'll find out when he gets served."

****

Darius expected the house to be still but not funeral parlor quiet. After disagreement number nine-hundred-ninety-nine, Melissa kept her distance. Staying in the bedroom or shoving her nose in a book whenever he walked in on her. Seeing her disappointment every time they talked, weighed on him. Everyone wanted a piece of him. Dan wanted his success because it lined his pocket with money. Melissa wanted time, which he couldn't manufacture, and his family wanted him to make music. Trying to remember what he wanted was becoming harder and harder to do. Sometimes it seemed unimportant.

His thoughts settled on his father. Mr. Randall Bellamy, the self-made millionaire, didn't understand why his son wasn't the biggest musical artist in the world by now. Everything Randall touched was a mega success, except his marriage. Maybe focusing on business was the way his father chose to bury all the other disappointments life had placed at his feet. He knew growing up in the middle of his parents' constant war had left him damaged. As much as he wanted to believe his marriage to Melissa was different, there was always an inkling nagging at him. Warning him that Melissa would crush him like his mother had crushed his father.

He dropped the car keys in the bowl designated for them. Another full night in the studio and only one step closer to finishing the last two tracks. He ran his hand down his face.

With the house all to himself, now was a good time to blast his record player. He selected a Sade album and placed the vinyl on the turntable. A few minutes without arguing or the forced silence filled with meaning was a relief. Melissa's sullenness was more deadly. At least the arguing was filled with passion. The cold detachment she now displayed could mean anything. Was Melissa giving up?

Winning a Grammy, going on worldwide tours, and having fans shout his name as he walked down the street were all grand, but the price was much higher than he could have ever guessed.

He flopped on the couch and crossed his ankle over his knee. With his head against the cushion, he closed his eyes. The virtual tug of war between him and Melissa rested on his chest, making it impossible to relax. The whimper from his new best friend caught his attention.

"I'm coming, boy," Darius said. As soon as he opened the crate, the puppy charged him, catching him off guard.

It was time to shake up his life. To snatch back the reins Dan insisted on holding and controlling. Now was the time for him to mold something familiar for himself. Now was time for the life he and Melissa used to dream about when they lived in the small walk-up they shared with ants and an upstairs neighbor who insisted on blaring his television at two in the morning.

The odor in the kitchen outranked a sewer. Between the dog's crate and the dishes caked with food, he wasn't sure which was worse.

"You must be pretty rugged to put up with this life." He walked the dog outside into the patch of land they called a back yard. As soon as his feet touched the overgrown grass, the dog bounded from one patch to another, sniffing his new freedom before turning to stand next to Darius.

"I think it's time we get a name for you," Darius petted the puffy. "How about Turk? Do you think you'd like to be called Turk?"

The dog licked his face. "No, it sounds too much like turd. How 'bout Turbo? It sounds better than Turk, doesn't it?"

Turbo ran around the yard as if he were happy to finally have an identity. Happy to have a home. Happy to have a family. Darius's chest constricted. He gasped for air. Those same things should have been enough to make him happy.

"How about we go inside and clean up the mess. Enough is enough. It's time I stop being a jerk."

Chapter Five

Melissa pressed her lips into a smile and unlocked the front door to the house. She tried to forget the comments the lawyer had felt compelled to point out, as if she were an idiot. Everything they had belonged to Darius. The duplex, the money, the cars, even the credit cards were in his name. According to the lawyer, for a woman her age, she hadn't accumulated much wealth. Even though in a divorce that wouldn't matter, she still felt like crap. The snappish attitude from the receptionist hadn't improved the mood of the meeting either.

What she wanted from Darius couldn't be purchased. She couldn't put the love she needed into his heart. Without the same level of commitment from him, it was time to fold, regardless of what she got to keep and what she had to walk away from. She'd come to San Francisco on a promise. Darius had vowed he'd make each day better than the one before and she'd been happy with his commitment. But his affirmation was now faded and frayed like an old newspaper.

As she stepped over the threshold into the house, it was obvious something was different. She remained still for several moments trying to detect the change. The current running through the residence had switched to a different frequency. She inhaled. The stench occupying the house like ghosts was missing.

She pulled the expensive Birkin bag purchased with Darius's hard-earned money from her shoulder and placed it on the table to investigate what was going on.

The dog ran to greet her. His tail wagged with force. "Hey, boy. What are you doing out of your crate?" She rubbed under his chin. Then patted the top of his head. He bumped her hand before trotting ahead of her into the kitchen.

Darius stood at the sink. From behind, he could have been any happy husband waiting on his wife to come home. But she knew better. There wasn't a soiled dish in sight. The stainless steel rim of the sink was visible for the first time since she'd returned from Bristol. The foul odor was gone along with the doggy crate.

"So, what's this all about?" Melissa leaned against the opening to the room, keeping enough distance between them in case he said anything out of line. The last thing she needed was another harsh word. She'd heard enough of them for one day.

"It was time, don't you think?" His smile drew her into the kitchen and onto the stool.

"Yeah, but I'm surprised just the same. Pleasantly surprised. I thought I was going to have to throw a stick of dynamite in here to clear this mess." She managed a smile.

He took the seat next to her. "He's got a name, finally." He nodded to the dog.

"A name, huh?" She rubbed the dog's head without taking her eyes off Darius. He seemed more relaxed. The tension between his brows was gone. Her heart swelled with emotion. The way she felt about him would never change, no matter what.

"Melissa, meet Turbo." He held his hand palm up. "Turbo, please meet my beautiful wife, Melissa."

She tickled the dog's neck. "Well, it's nice to meet you, Turbo. I guess you're an official member of the Bellamy family now that you have a real name."

For the first time in weeks, they sat together in a comfortable silence. It was like old times, when just being in the room with Darius was good enough. The only thing needed to make the memory more vivid was for him to hum a melody composed just for her.

"So, why did you do it?" she asked again.

"Do what?"

"Clean up the kitchen. I thought this was going to be your last stand, like Custer."

"What do you mean? You do know Custer died at Little Big Horn?"

"I thought you'd rather die than clean up the mess you made."

"I was being a jerk."

Melissa snorted. "But why?"

"If I knew why I did everything I did, I'd have all the answers." He rested his hand on her leg, above her knee. The familiar gesture had the traditional effect. Her body warmed. But her pride stuck in her throat, refusing to allow happiness to take hold or to admit she welcomed his touch. She pulled away and walked to the refrigerator.

After pouring a tumbler of water from the pitcher, she leaned against the counter opposite him. The distance gave her room to think.

Turbo settled on the floor between them as if deciding which side to take was too strenuous. He placed his head on top of his paws, his eyes cast up at her.

"Where have you been all day?" Darius's stare made her uneasy. "I tried to reach you on your cell."

She shrugged her shoulders. Nothing had been finalized today, so there wasn't anything to tell him yet. The lawyer wanted her to think it over, decide what she wanted. She cleared her throat. "Out. I had lots of errands to run. You know…for school and stuff."

He looked at his watch. "It's almost eleven o'clock. You must have had a lot to do."

"I stopped off at Pam's. We had dinner and spent some time talking. Why are you giving me the third degree?" She took a gulp of water.

"I'm not. I'm just asking. How are your classes? School starts this week, right?"

She took another sip of water and nodded. "Classes are fine. This semester I've got some students who want to get their money's worth." She set the glass down, glad the conversation had changed directions. But not yet ready to tell him she was bored with lesson plans, term papers, and final exams. Being an art history professor had sounded glamorous once upon a time, but now, the thought of spending her life at a dry erase board made her crazy. The same routine every day seemed like a long road with no landscaping. She wanted excitement and versatility, which wasn't on any syllabus she'd created.

"I'm surprised you asked. You're not usually interested in what I'm doing."

"Please don't lump my behavior into one category. I'm never all one thing or another. I think what you do is great. I admire your ability to stand in front of a classroom of college kids. You enjoy it so much. There's no self-doubt or worry if you're pleasing the right people."

"Oh, I have my doubts. Some days more than others."

Maybe Darius wasn't the bad guy. She seemed to have her share of secrets. She focused on the dog as he licked the pads of his paw.

Darius pushed off the stool and opened the refrigerator. The slight pop as he opened another one of his ever-present energy drinks made the dog raise his head.

"Why do you drink so many of those things?"

He examined the small bright bottle. "I don't know. I think it's a habit now and I like the taste."

She regarded him without replying. What had caused her serious, determined husband to become a complete stranger? Who had pulled away first, him or her? To patch up their life seemed impossible. She was weary just thinking about the amount of effort required. He was so focused on his music he didn't notice anything. Not her, not their marriage, not even what he consumed. She was living with a ghost. She heard him in the house, but she couldn't connect with him. The thought pierced her heart. It was like watching a tragedy unfolding and not being able to stop the destruction.

Her mind started forming the sentences to tell him about her visit to the lawyer's office. She rearranged the subject and predicated several different ways but her mouth couldn't speak the words. Not yet.

****

Darius drained the drink and dropped the empty container in the trash. "Why are you staring?" he asked.

She blinked and shook her head. "No reason. I'm just tired. I had a long day. I'm going to bed." She stood. "Goodnight." She headed through the door leading to the sun room. He heard her heels on the hardwood floor before she ascended the stairs.

He cracked his knuckles, then pressed his fingers backwards. Turbo stretched before sticking his nose in the air. The dog paced the path Melissa had followed as if signaling Darius to pursue her. They used to go to bed together every night. The highlight of their day was curling up together in bed and exploring each other's body. Maybe the memory was only an illusion. Had it been as blissful as he wanted to believe? Whatever was going on with Melissa carried on below the surface, in the part of her no one saw.

Touching her leg, even though it was only for a few seconds, reminded him of everything he missed. Melissa remained the center of his life, but convincing her of how important she was seemed impossible. Wanting his wife and his music wasn't asking too much. In the beginning, he'd convinced himself he could have it all, but now, there were doubts. He yearned for the simplicity of their early days of marriage, when it was just the two of them enclosed in a perfect bubble and not giving a damn about the outside world. He hadn't had his wife in weeks and his body reminded him of the absence like a nagging toothache.

He took the stairs two at a time, with the puppy right behind him, his claws clicking on the steps like a pair of tap shoes. Together, they sounded like a herd of buffalo charging the fort.

Outside the master bedroom, he held the doorknob and braced for the onslaught of anger she'd throw at him for invading her privacy the moment he crossed the sill.

Without overthinking what to do, he made his way past the walk-in closet into the opening of the room. She was propped on the bed, naked, rubbing lotion onto her arms.

"What are you doing in here?" Instead of the displeasure he expected, there was only curiosity in her tone. Turbo rushed to her side and hurled himself onto the bed. "Darius, if Trek or Turkey urinates or chews on any of my shoes, I'm going to throw you both out of here."

She jumped off the bed, gathering the towel around her breasts, and closed the closet door with a thud.

"It's Turbo, and he's not going to mess with your precious footwear. I had a long talk with him." He waved his hand. "Anyway, do I need to make a formal request to talk to my wife? Do you have a scheduling secretary I should talk to?"

She lifted a brow and settled back on the bed. "You've been so busy I thought you'd forgotten the fine art of discussion. Why are you so talkative tonight? What's going on, Darius?"

"We've both been busy." He regretted his tone the moment the words left his mouth. Defending his behavior made his chest constrict. He needed no one's approval for what he wanted to accomplish. He had enough money to buy several small record labels, but getting into the business the old fashion way, with hard work and talent, was the only thing important enough to matter. And he planned to get the movie score the same way.

"You've been coming home pretty late, but we can talk now," he said.

"I can't stand the empty house, so I stopped rushing home. I find I'm less irritable if I'm not sitting around waiting for you." She pumped lotion into her palm and ran her hand along her thigh. Her silky skin glistened. He curled his fingers into a fist to keep from reaching for her.

"Can you please close your legs a little more?" He looked away from the excellent view, but only for a second.

"I could, or you could leave my room. I'm getting ready to go to sleep." She nodded at the door.

At the edge of the bed, he pushed aside one of her frilly pillows and sat in front of her. Even though her forehead wrinkled, she continued the slow steady stroke along her leg.

"You're still staring," she said.

"The show keeps getting better and better. I can't stop watching. I haven't applied lotion to your back in a long time. Let me." He opened his hand for the bottle.

She hesitated for an instant before handing over the pump and turning her back to him. "Why tonight? What made you decide to help me now?"

"I used to do this all the time." His big hand on her small back swiped a wide path of moisturizer into her skin. Her flesh was supple. She arched her spine just enough to push her butt closer to him.

"Yeah, but that was a long time ago."

He moved up to her shoulders, applying pressure with his thumbs the way she liked. As much as he wanted to grab her ass, it would have been an instant invitation for him to leave the room. "I figured your back might be dry since I haven't done this in a while."

Her jovial huff was the only encouragement he needed to squirt more lotion into his hands. This time he slathered each side of her waist and brushed her breasts as he completed his tasks. The mellow fragrance pulled him away to the quick honeymoon they'd spent on Lake George before moving west. The long weekend was all laughs, food, and sex. A few years later and a few obstacles later, and now, they were more like strangers than lovers.

"I guess I owe you a pair of boots, don't I? We never had our shopping excursion."

Her shoulders tensed. "It's okay. I'll purchase them myself when I'm ready."

The reedy sound of her voice said what her words didn't. He heard the disappointment she tried to hide. His stomach rolled. He didn't want to be the cause of her unhappiness. His job was to make her euphoric.

"I want to buy them for you. I pay my debts." He tried to lighten the mood. Tonight, he wanted to hold her. Rubbing her back was sending his body crazy messages of pure delight.

"If we start listing all your debts, we won't get any sleep tonight."

"Then I better get started, don't 'cha think?"

Coming to her room had nothing to do with sex, but now, every cell in his body sang some version of a mating song. Making love to his wife should have been as natural as walking the dog, but his hands trembled as he ran them down her spine.

He drew closer to the tender curve of her neck, the sweet spot where he could always get her going.

"Don't, Darius." She spun around and clambered off the bed. The dog came to his feet and stretched his hindquarters.

"What? Don't do what, kiss my wife?" He stood too.

"We might be married, but we haven't lived in marital bliss in months. You do your thing and I've been doing mine. Just because you cleaned the kitchen doesn't change anything."

"I think we both had a hand in what's happening or not happening in our relationship. You used to be my biggest supporter, but I'm not feeling the love anymore."

Her shoulders rose and fell as she took a deep breath. "You sound as if I abandoned you. But you deserted me long before I stopped cheering."

"I didn't mean to."

"We sleep in separate bedrooms, and a day at the office for you could be a make out session with some groupie."

His right eye twitched. "I've never made out with another woman and you know it. You're mad at the world for some reason and you just like to place all the blame on me. I'm not your father and I haven't cheated on you."

"My father has nothing to do with us."

The venom in her words should have backed him against the wall but the hurt in her eyes was the only thing he saw. Without hesitating, he opened his arms and pulled her compact body closer. She tried to pull away, wrenching her shoulder against his chest, but instead of releasing her, he tightened his hold.

"Melissa, I'm not your enemy. You might not like the way I'm going about my career, but don't question my love for you. I've never stepped outside of my marriage and I never will. I've always laid everything on the line for you. I just need you to stick with me. Together, we can make this work." He nuzzled her closer.

"Darius, I can't live my life on hold while you're doing your thing."

"It's what we agreed when we moved here. What's different now?"

She twisted away from him, harder this time. "I am."

Chapter Six

Melissa avoided looking at Darius as he stormed out of the bedroom with Turbo at his heels. As he slammed the door, sadness spread through her like a warm summer rain moving across a dry field.

Melissa climbed into the king-sized bed and pulled the pale pink sheet to her chin. With no energy to fight the inevitable, she allowed the melancholy back into all the familiar places. Their house had turned into her parents' home. From the outside, everything appeared perfect and happy. But inside, the rage and words they flung at each other could sink a ship.

Of course, she'd be the one to follow in her mother's footsteps. Fate was having a really good laugh at her for sticking her nose in the air and admonishing her mother for putting up with their father's antics. It was so easy to advise her mother to get a divorce and get on with her life. Now, she needed someone to give her the same kick in the ass.

But love had a firm grip on her heart. Just having Darius touch her was enough to make her acquiesce to whatever he wanted. Which explained why they were living his life and not their life.

The familiar brush of his slightly rough hand on her back had sent a wake-up message through her body. Her heart pounded in her chest and the tingle between her legs wouldn't allow sleep to take her. Damn him for making her want what she wouldn't allow herself to have.

She slid to the edge of the bed and dialed her sister. Even with the time distance, maybe Dakota would be awake.

When her sister picked up, Melissa said, "I know it's late there but I needed to talk to someone."

"No, no, it's fine. Are you okay?" Dakota asked. Her voice was laced with sleep.

"Did I wake you and Bishop?"

"Girl, a bomb could go off in the living room and Bishop would sleep through it. But you haven't answered my question. Asa told me you were seeing a lawyer."

"I figured she would. And I did." Melissa paused. "I'm so torn. I know what I need to do. It's just so hard to do. I still love him and it hurts so much."

"Love isn't supposed to hurt, honey." Dakota's voice softened. "But if you have any uncertainty, then you should wait. Don't do something you might regret."

"Dakota, you know how I am. I can't sit on my hands and hope things will get better. I'm not like Mom. I won't accept morsels of attention doled out by

Darius like precious stones. Maybe accepting infidelity and a child out of wedlock worked for Mom, but not for me."

"You don't know if Mom ever accepted any such thing. No one does. But you can't live your life based on what you thought Mom did or didn't do. Has he cheated on you?"

Melissa fingered the scalloped edge of the sheet and bit back the tears. "I don't know for sure. But it certainly feels like it."

"So, you've convicted him without any real evidence?"

Melissa huffed. "Even if he's not cheating, he wants me to stay hidden like I'm too ugly to show in public. He's living this glamorous life and I get to sit home and eat dinner alone."

After a long silence, Dakota said, "Asa and I are coming for a visit. She should be able to fly since she's only a few months pregnant."

"No, you guys don't need to come. I'll be fine. It's just he came in the bedroom tonight and it was so normal. It was like old times."

"When I come, we'll do a cleansing. Maybe your house needs a new aura. I found a new, heartier sage."

"Oh please, Dakota. I wish it were as simple as a little herb therapy. Go back to sleep. I'll call in a few days."

"We're coming to see you, Melissa," Dakota repeated before hanging up the phone.

Melissa set the receiver back on the base and snuggled under the covers. God bless Mim and Pepe. One of her grandparents' lasting legacies, which dwelled deep in the Conroy family, was the love of family. No matter what was going on, her sisters would be there for her.

Melissa drummed her fingers on the notepad beside the bed. Everything she needed to get done in the next few days was listed. The one thing not on the list was *what to do if you're unhappy*. How could she have forgotten to make a Plan B? She'd fussed at her sisters for dodging responsibility, only to fall into the same chasm herself.

Tears gathered in her eyes as her throat constricted with pain. Giving up the fight, she allowed reality to wash over her, accepting every bitter morsel. With the sheet over her head, she released the loud sob she'd been trying to suppress for weeks.

Within minutes Darius was back. "Melissa, are you okay?" Darius asked.

She caught her breath, freezing the whimper in her chest. How long had he been listening to her cry?

"I'm fine, Darius. Fine."

The mattress sank under his weight as he climbed into bed and gathered her sheet-encased body in his arms. "You're not fine, you're crying."

"What are you doing, spying on me?"

"I was taking the dog outside. I heard you."

"I'm fine, just leave me alone, please."

He tightened his hold and rocked her with a tenderness they hadn't experienced in over a year. She could exhale and allow him to soothe her, but one night of tenderness wouldn't wipe away the brokenness.

She pushed the sheet away from her face but kept her back to him. "I said I'm fine, Darius." She smelled the cool night air in the fibers of his clothes.

"You don't sound fine." Darius pressed his lips against her neck. His warm breath across her skin beckoned her dormant libido. He ran his hand down her arm and over her hips, caressing her along the way. Just feeling his touch heated every bit of her body, driving away the resistance she used to protect herself.

With his index finger, Darius turned her head. His kiss was so tender, her body wilted. All the tension, anger, and resentment collecting under her skin like falling leaves against a fence blew away when his tongue seized hers.

She shifted to face him. His eyes were dark with desire. Darius trailed kisses along her cheek, down her neck, and settled into her collarbone. Each one was hotter than the one before. Melissa pushed the sheet away from her naked body to allow the heat to escape.

"We haven't made love in months. Did you know it was that long ago?" His voice was heavy with lust.

"I know." Melissa slipped her hand behind his neck to draw him closer.

"You have got to be the sexiest woman I know." He cupped her breasts with the palms of his hands, taking turns kissing each nipple. "Do you know how hard it's been for me to stay away from you?"

"I've never asked you to stay away." Melissa stopped his hand.

"You didn't say the words, but the meaning was there." He pulled his hand free and rested it on her belly. The sexual energy between them was lightening hot. Ignoring it wasn't an option. Her body screamed for him.

"Get undressed, please." She tugged at the button on his shirt.

Darius pushed off the bed and lifted his shirt over his head. He twisted the snap on his jeans and pushed them down his legs. The sight of his strong, muscular body was enough to erase the last of her resolve. Whatever they needed to discuss could be handled another time. The only thing making sense now was the fervor taking over her body.

He crawled back into bed, between her legs, covering her body with his. The familiar scent of his skin and touch was like a welcome home party. It felt good to be back in his arms, even if it was only for a moment. She wrapped her arms around his back and deeply rubbed the surface of each muscle. Each one more familiar than the last.

His shaft pushed against her thigh with the same urgency that her core shrieked for him. For the rest of her life her body would probably call out for Darius in the wee hours of the morning when the loneliness pressed down on her like a boulder.

The scruff of his late night stubble tickled her neck, shocking reality back into her head. Guilt invaded her pleasure. Her body stiffened, her senses locked down.

"What's wrong?" He pulled back and surveyed her.

She shook her head and shoved his shoulder away. "I'm not doing this, Darius. I'm not making love to you tonight or any other night. We do this every time, gloss over the elephant in the room, and the only person who gets screwed is me."

"What elephant? What are you talking about?" He stuck out his chest in the familiar indignant manner he always adopted when he thought he was being attacked.

"Aren't you just horny tonight? And I'm the only available female, so I'll do."

He huffed and moved to the edge of the bed. "Why the hell did you pretend you would?" He snatched his pants and shirt off the floor with a violent jerk and stormed out of the room. Instead of following him, the dog jumped on the foot of the bed and buried his muzzle on his paws.

"Come on, Turbo, before she turns you against me too," Darius yelled from the other end of the hall.

The dog looked back at her before leaping down and trotting out the door.

****

No matter how many ways he dissected the events of last night, he kept coming up blank. Trying to sleep with a dick as hard as a telephone pole was like trying to sleep in the middle of Fisherman's Wharf on a Saturday afternoon. Darius buried his head in his hand and rubbed his face hard. Their marriage needed work, way more than he'd estimated.

Rain pelted the kitchen windows. From the stool, he could see clear blue sky off in the distance. It was going to be one of those days that required his patience until the clouds moved off to ruin someone else's plans.

He pulled bacon and eggs from the refrigerator along with an energy drink. In a matter of minutes, the smell of cooking bacon filled the house, bringing the dog sniffing into the kitchen. Now, all it had to do was work on Melissa the way it worked on Turbo, and he might pull off his plan.

Once breakfast was ready, he set the table with the white, ceramic, every day china Melissa loved.

"Are you coming down for breakfast?" he yelled from the base of the stairs.

She opened the bedroom door. "You cooked for me?"

"Of course. It's ready. Come on down."

She placed her hands on her hips. Today, she wore a pair of faded jeans and a chunky sweater. She pursed her lips together and hesitated for a moment before saying, "I'll be right there."

By the time Melissa walked into the kitchen, the rain had stopped and a hint of sunlight peeked through the window. He leaned over the sink to push the window open. The crisp air lifted the curtains.

"When did you start watching Sunny Kincaid's morning gossip show?" She pointed to the television pushed into the corner of the counter. The studio audience was clapping and chanting the talk show host's name.

"She doesn't just do gossip. If you want to know what's going on in the entertainment industry, she's the one you better tune in. She knows everything."

"Doesn't Dan keep you informed?"

"Yeah, but he gets his information off the show too. This way I don't have to listen to his translation." He paused to observe Melissa. "Why are you looking at me like you've never seen me before?"

"I didn't know you watched this show. Dakota had it on every morning and I had to listen to her and Asa talk about it for hours. The two of them were going to get tickets for a taping in New York."

"I don't think I'd want to sit in the audience. I just want to know what's happening in the industry. Now, let's eat before breakfast gets cold."

"I'm surprised you cooked. What's this all about?" She sat at the table.

"Let's just say I couldn't sleep. I had a bad case of blue balls, so I decided I might as well make myself useful."

She smiled and bit a piece of bacon. "I think we both had the same problem. Welcome to my club."

"You could have saved the both of us from a painful night."

"Yeah, but then I wouldn't have gotten breakfast."

"What are your plans for today? I'd like to kidnap you."

She pushed the food around on her plate while eyeing him. "What have you got in mind?"

"Just go with it, Melissa. You don't have to know everything. Trust me."

She twisted her mouth into a frown. "I'm not trying to be difficult, but tell me why I should trust my day in your hands. As soon as Dan calls, you'll drop me like a bad habit and go running."

"Are you going to give it a try or not?" He pressed his face close to hers.

The kitchen clock ticked so loud it drowned out the street noise. Each second tick pushed them further apart. Either she was holding her breath or her breathing was so soft it was soundless. When she didn't reply, he said, "We're leaving the house in ten minutes. Be ready."

Chapter Seven

The drive was peaceful. Melissa needed a day without the constant rancor. She tapped her tongue against her inside bottom lip. Granted, she and Darius hadn't spent any time together in months, but one afternoon of attention wouldn't save their marriage. The air was leaking out of their relationship, and instead of patching up the holes, they continued to chink at the armor that was supposed to hold them together.

From the corner of her eye, she observed his dark glasses and the baseball cap pulled down snug on his head. His face was hardly recognizable.

"Expecting trouble?" she asked.

He touched the brim of his hat. "No, but I don't want anyone interrupting our time together. No autographs or demo tapes today."

"And what about Dan? Do you think he can manage without you for one full day?"

He lifted his phone from the breast pocket of his jacket and turned it off. "No Dan today either."

"I'm impressed," she said without suppressing her smile. Darius had never before tuned Dan out or put her in front of his business schedule.

He chuckled. "Well, good. I haven't been able to impress you in a long time."

A comfortable silence filled the interior of the car. Melissa folded her hands in her lap. Maybe today wouldn't be so bad. They used to spend Saturdays together schlepping around, doing the tourist thing, and eating pounds of junk food. At night, they'd fall into bed with their bags scattered at the foot. Everything was funny then, he could make her laugh with the most mundane statements. She hadn't dissolved into laughter since she'd left her sisters in Bristol.

"Can you tell me what we're going to do today?" Melissa hoped she didn't sound like a control freak who couldn't go with the flow or show spontaneity. Even though his gesture was nice, it was time for her to find her way. Maybe moving back to Bristol would improve her life. It seemed to be working well for both Asa and Dakota. She had enough attitude to gather the reigns of her life. How hard could it be?

"You're not going to be happy until I tell you, right? Okay." He paused as he pulled into a parking garage in Nob Hill. "This is just a spur-of-the-moment outing, so I thought I'd take you to your favorite shoe store in all the world, and then we could have a late lunch at your favorite place down on the wharf."

"You mean McCormick and Kuleto's?"

He pulled into an open space and turned off the car. "Yep, you know the one." He hopped out of the car and opened her door.

Without asking, he slipped his hand around hers and led her onto the crowded street.

"First things first. I owe you a pair of expensive boots, don't I?"

"That train left the station weeks ago. Remember? Let's not put it back on the tracks." She pretended to scratch her arm so he would release her hand. To buy the shoes now would be like getting a birthday gift six months late. The gesture would be nice, but there wouldn't be any thrill. If she kept falling for his charm, then she deserved all the unhappiness that visited her. Carrying the box around Nob Hill, pretending to be a happily married couple would only mark how low they had sunk. Darius was used to getting everything he wanted. The silver spoon in his mouth was a small part of his family keepsakes. There was a time when he thought he wanted her. The way he'd kept showing up on her parents' doorstep, even though she'd spent most of her day ignoring him, had finally worn her down. He had spun a wonderful tale of what their lives would be like in California. She couldn't help but place her heart on the closest thing to a silver platter available and hand it over to him.

Not a smart move. Now, all she needed was a seat on one of those salacious daytime talk shows to discuss how gullible she had been. Putting everything on hold just for him.

Melissa slowed her gait. "I'd really like to pick up some loose teas while we're in Chinatown." She turned in the opposite direction. The small gesture to take control of life made her feel better.

"Are you sure? I thought you ordered your teas online."

She picked up her pace. The more distance she put between her and shoe shopping, the less pity churned in her stomach.

In the small, cramped teashop, she tasted a few sample brews and smelled several varieties before selecting the sweet-scented Oolong and a dark Rooibos. Instead of glancing at his watch or checking his cell phone, Darius stood by her side, tasting and sampling alongside her. While he poured on the charm, she had to step higher or drown in the pool of make-believe.

Two young girls stepped into the shop, their heads bent as they giggled in each other's ear. They didn't look old enough to be out without parents, but each wore impeccable make-up.

The tallest preteen shrieked and pointed. "Look, it's Darius B!" She shrieked again and added a jump to punctuate the sound.

The two of them began to squeal and slapped each other's hands.

"You might as well give them your autograph before they pass out." Melissa tried to sound casual. Young girls weren't the issue. It was the women who simpered around him and wanted more than his signature that caused the riffs.

After snapping pictures with the most sophisticated cell phones Melissa had ever seen, Darius signed a piece of paper provided by the shop owner. Both girls left the store giggling harder than when they walked in.

"Where to now?" Darius asked after she made her purchase and they stepped back onto the crowded, narrow street. "Tell you what, since our dinner reservation isn't until later, how about I buy you a corn dog to hold you until then?"

"I think I'll pass. While you're eating your wiener, I'll get some chocolate."

"Deal." He wrapped his arm around her waist and steered her towards the wharf. She didn't want to be happy, but she was.

****

Hand-in-hand, they climbed the stairs to McCormick and Kuleto; Darius didn't try to downplay the jocularity he felt. It was the best time he'd had in months.

"Are you hungry?" He held her by the waist as they waited for the hostess to return to the desk.

"I am. After so much walking, I'm famished." She held up her bag. "And I saved some chocolate for dessert."

"You'll share with me, won't you?"

"I'll think about it." She gave him her prettiest smile. The same one he'd fallen in love with and hadn't seen since she'd returned from Delaware. All he'd seen was the half smile she had adopted. Actually, it was a cross between a smile and a sneer.

The blonde hostess bounced to the podium. "You're Darius, the singer, aren't you?" The hostess placed her hand on top of his and licked her glossy lip. This freight train needed to be stopped now.

He pulled his hand away. "Is our table ready?"

"Yes, of course. If you'll just follow me." She picked up a couple of menus and led them to a table. "Please let me know if you need anything. Anything at all," she said, before walking away.

Melissa clucked and held her hands together.

No way was such a minor incident going to ruin the day. "Ignore her, please. It was nothing." He positioned Melissa's chair to see out the window. "Your favorite view. And look, the sun is setting."

She rested her chin in the palm of her hand while staring at the darkening purple and pink sky. "I do like sitting here and seeing Alcatraz. You'd think I'd get tired of looking at it, but…" She hunched her shoulders.

"I wanted our day to be perfect. We needed it."

"Well, you've outdone yourself. And we haven't said one cross word to each other all day. I think we have a new record."

He nodded. "Can I order for you?"

She put her menu down. For the briefest moment, everything was perfect.

Dinner flew by in a rush. Nothing slowed time no matter how long it took him to butter his bread or chew the lobster. His full stomach coiled with disappointment when the server placed the check in front of him. Her easy manner at dinner had left the door open just enough for him to push through. As soon as they got home, he'd planned to test her just a bit.

"I hope you enjoyed dinner," he said.

"I did. But I'm exhausted now."

"Thank you for coming today." He studied her face, happy to see a genuine smile.

She folded her napkin and placed it on the table before turning her gaze to the window. The only thing visible was the glare of distant lights in the dark sky. Even the outline of Alcatraz was hard to make out.

"Oh no, here she comes again." Melissa's eyes flared with anger.

The hostess rested her hand on his shoulder, lingering a moment too long. The heat from her hand penetrated his shirt. He shifted just enough to escape her touch.

"How was your dinner?" she asked.

Before he could respond, Melissa piped up. "Everything was delicious. Thank you for asking."

Without looking at Melissa, he could feel the tension settle over the table. It was the same tightness that existed in their house and in the words they spoke to each other. How silly he'd been to think they could escape reality for just one day. She didn't want to understand the games he needed to play in this industry. Being rude to fans could stall his career. If Dan had taught him nothing else, he'd drilled in the importance of connecting with the public. Always.

Instead of looking at Melissa, he focused his attention on the folio and paying the check. A business card fluttered to the floor like a butterfly in flight. Without seeing the details, he knew what it said. A phone number. An address. An invitation for a night of coitus. It wasn't the first time he'd received such an offer slipped to him in the most ridiculous ways. But in front of his wife—it caused his stomach to churn. He suppressed the urge to yell or call the manager. Now wasn't the time for his ego to control the situation. Melissa deserved respect and he wanted the hostess to give it to her, but Melissa would hate it if he made a scene.

Melissa plucked the card off the floor. "Don't look so surprised. She probably thinks I'm just the bimbo for the evening since nobody knows I'm your wife."

"Tonight is about you. I don't care what is going on in her head. I've never seen her before and I'll never see her again. Leave the card on the floor. That's where it belongs." He pushed away from the table. "I'm ready to take my beautiful wife home."

Melissa flipped the card onto the table as he secured his hand around her waist and escorted her out of the restaurant.

Chapter Eight

Melissa remembered when the most eventful part of their dates was the hot night of sex afterwards. Now, with his music so famous, whacky fans meant almost anything could happen, even in upscale places. She pushed her shoulders back and allowed Darius's hand to ride her waist as she exited the restaurant, and they made their way to the parking garage.

"It comes with the territory, Melissa," he said as he held the car door open for her.

"I know. I'm not saying a word. But I often wonder if you'd be as patient with me if I were the star and men were always in pursuit of me? Seriously, what would you do?"

She could almost see the thought scroll across his brain. He rested his hand on top of the car.

"I would do everything possible to help make your dream come true." His face darkened. Darius had a tinge of jealousy coursing through his veins like blood. There was no way he would tolerate half of the insolence or flirting that she put up with, and her patience was waning too.

"Your statement sounds like it's laced with qualifiers. You see, it's not as simple as it seems," she said.

"I know how difficult this situation is for you. And even though you might find this hard to believe, I don't like it either. But it won't be much longer, I promise you."

As she slid into the passenger seat, he rubbed his hand over her butt. Maybe he hoped she'd forget the incident in the restaurant. She'd try to make an effort to remain nonchalant. If he could handle what happened in the restaurant, then she certainly would find a way to get through the absurdity too. At least for one more night.

With her seatbelt secured, he closed the door and walked to the driver's side. After he got in the car and locked the door, she said, "If I wasn't with you tonight, what would you have done with the business card?" She contracted her stomach and waited for his reply. She sounded as insecure as a kid on the first day of school, but picking at the scab made her feel better.

"If you hadn't been sitting beside me, I would have called the manager. I think a hostess at a fine dining place should be used to seeing celebrities. But tonight, I was determined nothing was going to ruin our day, so I let her stupid behavior pass." He paused. "Why? What do you think I should have done?"

"I guess I wanted you to defend my honor or something archaic along those lines."

"This really bothers you, doesn't it, Melissa?"

"I thought I could do the famous life. The folks on talk shows make it sound so easy. You know I think I'm tough as nails. But yes, it gets to me and I can't get over how much you like the attention."

"I won't lie to you, the attention is nice, but not at your expense. I remember when we used to spend time together without going out of the house. Those times were better than anything."

"I thought you hated those days. You used to look like your skin was itching to break away from the confines of home."

"What I hated…never mind," he said.

"What? Finish your statement." A husband and wife shouldn't have to struggle so much to be happy. The constant need to tiptoe around his life and tamp down her emotions was exhausting. The weight of trying so hard left no energy to think about herself or her future. The sooner she told him about the divorce, the sooner she could mend her broken life, set her own direction without walking in his wake.

"I want to make my family proud. They've put their hopes and dreams on me and I feel like I owe them something."

Melissa shook her head. She understood the pressures of family.

"Darius, I need to talk to you about something."

"I need to tell you something too." He paid the parking attendant and pulled into the street. "I have to go to New York next week. My tour starts and it's scheduled to last several months. I'd ask you to come along for the first show but I know you can't miss school."

Instead of responding, she intertwined her fingers and held them tight. Refusing to say one harsh word that might change the direction of their night.

"School just started and you usually hate to miss class in the first couple of weeks. See, even when you think I'm not paying attention, I am." He looked so satisfied at being able to remember something, she bit down on her tongue to keep from telling him he was wrong.

He had no way of knowing how much she'd loved to travel with him. When she got the job at the university she'd made a big point of telling him how important her career was and how she couldn't go traipsing off with him to every concert or gathering. That tirade haunted her now.

Her stomach swirled like a cat chasing its tail. "Great," she managed over the big knot at the back of her throat.

"What did you have to tell me?"

"It was nothing." She closed her eyes and leaned back against the headrest. Telling him about the lawyer seemed less important now. His life was so wrapped around himself, he probably wouldn't even notice he was being served with divorce papers. *Perfection did not exist.* She'd have to remember those four words. Especially when her heart started to race with happy thoughts and grand illusions or when the familiar queasy feeling invaded her stomach.

Every night with Darius could be magical if she could close out the rest of the world and the people who wanted to share his life as though they could claim a piece of him.

She wanted the uncomplicated lives of her sisters. Where strangers didn't creep over the boundaries like willow tree roots.

They rode in silence for several miles. She snatched quick glimpses of Darius as he made his way through the late night traffic. The casual way he rested his hands on the bottom of the steering wheel set her at ease. She tried to clear away the runaway thoughts.

"Do you remember when we used to stay up all night, just talking?" she asked.

"Yes. Before we started spending the night arguing." He chuckled as he focused on the road.

He pulled the car under the porte-cochere and shut off the engine. Before getting out, he cupped her knee with his palm. "Thanks for not making a big deal out of what happened in the restaurant."

"I understand the groupies, the wannabes, and the moochers. What I don't understand is why I have to act like I don't exist."

"After the studio picks up the soundtrack for the movie. I'll make some changes. It won't be much longer."

"That's our new mantra, isn't it?"

"I mean it this time," he said.

Now was the time to tell him she'd talked to a lawyer about divorce, but it could be their last blissful day together. She still had until Monday to change her mind. On Tuesday, he would be served the papers and she planned to be on a plane back to Delaware.

Darius ran around the car and opened her door. Once inside the house, Turbo charged him.

"I need to take the dog for a walk. He's been cooped up all day." He reached for the leash.

"Good night, Darius. I'm going to bed. Thank you again for a lovely day." She kissed his full lips and then used her thumb to swipe away the gloss.

He grabbed her wrist. "Wait up for me. I want to talk. I'll only be a few minutes. Let me take the dog out." His eyes pleaded for her acceptance.

She nodded and ran up the stairs before he made another request she couldn't muster a reasonable objection to.

After taking a short, hot shower, the tension between her shoulders relaxed. She hummed a Jeffrey Osborne song her mother used to love. Whenever her mother was upset with her father, she would hum *We're Going All the Way*, as if by buzzing with the melody she could reinforce their marriage. Somewhere during her marriage, Melissa started doing the same thing. But the song didn't provide the comfort it seemed to bring her mother.

While Melissa slathered on her favorite Bvlgari moisturizer, she continued to hum. Then, she wrapped the towel around her back and tucked it tight above her breasts.

The tap on the door shook her serenity.

"Melissa, I'm coming in."

She opened the bathroom door to find him stretched across the bed. He reached into his pocket and removed an energy drink. The small, red bottle disappeared in his palm.

"Darius, I'm not dressed yet. Could you give me a minute to put on a gown?"

He patted the bed, slapping it with his palm. "You don't need to put on anything. You're beautiful."

His words hung in mid-air. For a moment, she wasn't sure what to do, grab the gown or follow his advice.

She checked the tuck of the towel before sitting next to him. Not only were her thighs exposed, her bare butt was inches away from the man who still held her heart. If he made half of a sexual attempt tonight, she didn't have the willpower to fend him off. She wanted him to touch her, wake up her body, and take it for a ride. "Please make yourself comfortable," She tried to sound sarcastic.

"I just did." He crossed his ankles. Even though he was fully dressed, her imagination started thinking about all the things they had done in their bed. Tonight would be perfect if they could have just one iota of that happiness again.

The fear of trying to act like a normal couple made it hard to breathe. The two of them sitting and talking should have been easy. But so much disappointment had passed between them, too much to be taken back. She wasn't sure where they'd begin.

She inched closer to him. "So, what do you want to talk about?" she asked while pretending to examine her pedicure.

"Nothing specific. We haven't really chatted in a long time." He crossed his arms. "The night is still young and so are you. I'd thought I'd enjoy both."

"What a cheesy line. Let's hope you write better lyrics."

"You know I do." He dropped his leg over hers. Even through his slacks, she could feel the heat from his limb.

"I know no such thing." She chuckled.

He placed her in a bear hug, which only made her laugh harder. The delicious feel of being in his arms sent all her trepidations scurrying. She held him tight. The heft of his body pressing her into the mattress was as familiar as his touch and smell.

His hand slipped behind her neck and pulled her closer. She brushed her lips across his. The moment they connected, her heart started knocking in her chest. When his tongue darted into her mouth, for an instant, she wanted to protest, but the emptiness in her heart overpowered her reasoning. Like butter, her body melted, submitting to the desire to have him. She crushed her mouth hard against his.

This was wrong and she knew it. One signature away from filing for divorce and the two of them were embracing like lovers on a honeymoon. Even though her brain was trying to sort out what was happening, her body surged ahead of her reasoning and she ran her hand under his T-shirt. Her fingers greeted every tight muscle along his back, like welcoming an old friend she hadn't seen in a while.

The towel bunched around her waist, leaving her breasts exposed. He rubbed his palm over one nipple, then the next. The small circles made them stand at attention, demanding to be touched.

For the first time in months, she felt alive. His touch stroked her to awareness, filling her with anticipation. The love she held for him made the moment right. Any hesitation she harbored about giving her body to him vanished as his breath brushed over her neck and shoulders. For once, she didn't want to be reasonable or prudent, she only wanted to be loved by the man who occupied her heart. She parted her legs as he pushed between her thighs. The fabric from his slacks roughed her skin.

"Are you going to undress?" Her voice rushed out thick and husky.

He kissed her while slipping out of his shirt. He pulled the sleeve free without releasing her mouth. She unbuckled his belt and guided his pants over his solid thighs. The moment he was completely undressed, he freed the knot in the towel exposing her damp flesh.

For several moments, his eyes swept over her body, as if he were preparing to devour her. The gleam on his face said the Darius she married wanted her. She allowed her hand to drift down his body, relishing every muscle along the way. When she reached his swollen member, she tightened her fingers around it and massaged him slowly.

"Oh, baby," he whispered.

"Yes."

"Nobody can do what you do to my body," he responded between gasps.

"You taught me everything I know." She flashed to the first time she gave her body to Darius. His tender touch had made her first experience one worth cherishing, unlike her girlfriends who'd complained about the fumbling, bumbling, and pain of losing their virginity. She continued to fondle his shaft. With his eyes closed he inserted his finger between her moist folds. The sensation forced her back off the bed, against his flat stomach and chest.

Swallowed up in the ecstasy, she dangled from a string she couldn't cut. For several moments, she luxuriated between consciousness and unconsciousness. There wasn't any room for sadness in the rhapsody enveloping her. When her body was pressed to the limits, she surrendered to the explosion ricocheting through her loins.

****

Darius waited for her breathing to return to normal before shifting his weight. With his arms wrapped tightly around her, he pulled her closer.

Filling his nostrils with her scent. The longing waned enough to allow him to take a deep breath.

"We belong together." He spoke into the soft curve of her neck. "You should know how important you are to me."

"I want to. But we need more than one peaceful night."

"I took you for granted. I know better now." He pressed his lips into the flesh of her neck.

"I think we're both guilty of the same crime. In the beginning, I was so busy enjoying the good life, the cars, the nice house, the designer clothes. I didn't even know how lonely I was. But seeing the joy my sisters have with their partners makes me feel isolated, like I sold my soul. I think we deserve more."

"What do you really want? I'd give you the world if it would make you happy."

Her hand slipped over his arm. "I just want us to be happy. Sit down to dinner at night. Watch movies on television. Hold hands while walking down the street. I want to know I can count on you and you'll be there. Not just some of the time, but all the time." She climbed on top of him and planted kisses along his chest, down his abdomen.

"You got it, babe." He managed to say as she took his swollen shaft in her mouth. "You got it." His voice was barely audible as she pushed reality away with her skillful tongue.

He clutched the sheets in his palms to keep from pulling her hair. Sex with Melissa was always over the moon, but tonight there was desperation. He needed her to fill him up, put him back together again. But he couldn't show that kind of vulnerability. If she didn't believe in him, he had nothing.

He conceded his failings and focused on the pleasure she offered. Being a success would be worthless if Melissa wasn't in his life. He'd find a way to secure her by his side.

With his hands under her arms, he pulled her up. In a swift move, he climbed on top of her and pushed inside. "This is what I need. He buried his stiff rod inside of her.

Melissa locked her legs around his back, drawing him deeper. The warmth of her body, inside and out, drove his temperature up. Her hips ground against his with an urgency that demanded a matching rhythm. The slow, steady motion welded them into the single soul they used to be.

For the last few years, he had been so focused on the music; he'd sat Melissa on a shelf and expected her not to expire until he returned to collect her from her pedestal. A foolish notion believing so little would satisfy her.

He tucked his head to kiss her forehead, her cheeks, and her mouth. This time instead of just saying the words, he needed to give her more. Show her she was the priority.

She pulled her legs tighter, signaling she was close to the brink again.

"Now, baby," he spoke in her ear.

All of his blood seemed to pool in his loins, the throbbing mounted with each thrust. He burrowed deep as his body shuddered, each one bigger and more intense than the last, until an explosion claimed him, ripping him away from the real world and into ecstasy.

His body rocked with pleasure for several moments before the tide released him.

"You don't have any idea how much I missed you." He continued to hold her.

"Maybe just as much as I've been missing you." She stared into his eyes. She sighed like a weight rested on her chest. "How did we end up here?"

"By not paying attention and taking each other for granted." He rolled away and folded her into the crease of his arm. "I don't leave for New York for a while. Let's get away. Just you and me."

"But what about school?" Even though she protested, her tone indicated she was willing.

"You never take any time off work. Tell them it's an emergency. Tell them you need some time to finish your book. Tell them anything. Say you'll come away with me."

She pushed up on her elbow and looked down on him. "Don't tease me, Darius, or I just might take you up on your offer."

He grabbed her arm. "Melissa, I'm dead serious. I've never wanted to take you away so badly."

"Where will we go on such short notice?"

"Hawaii. Let's go to Maui. I'll have all the arrangements made tomorrow morning. We can leave in a day or two. What do you say?" He spoke fast while she was still contemplating the idea.

She nodded slowly.

"This can be the honeymoon we never had. Are you game?"

She sat straight up in the bed now. From the glint in her eye, he could tell the idea was taking hold of her. "Okay. Let's do it." She jumped off the bed. "But I'm not sure I have everything I need. What about a bathing suit? I can't get everything squared away so fast."

He pulled her back into bed. The sparkle in her eyes resembled diamonds in sunlight. The only thing important was the two of them. "We'll buy whatever we need when we get there. Now, how about giving me some more loving?"

She crawled on top of him, straddling his hips with her thighs. His body jerked to attention. "I'm going to wear you out."

"God, I hope so." He pulled her down on top of his erect shaft.

Chapter Nine

Last night was perfect. Getting out of bed might break the spell. Melissa turned toward Darius. Even though his eyes were closed, she knew he wasn't asleep. Maybe he had the same reluctance of changing the current flawless tableau.

"I know you're awake, so stop pretending." She pushed her finger into his chest.

His hand slid down and gripped her butt. "You're right, but I haven't been this relaxed in weeks. This is better than a sedative." He paused. "I love you, Melissa."

"Keep telling me. Don't miss a day." She trailed her finger up and down his chest.

"What will I get in return?" He nuzzled closer to her.

"We'll get to be happily married for the rest of our lives. We can grow old together. I'll even push your wheelchair on stage when you accept your Lifetime Achievement Award." She laughed.

"Why do I have to be in a wheelchair?"

"I'm just saying." Her laughter turned into full out giggles as he tickled her neck. She rolled out of bed onto the floor to get away from him. The dog started to bark from the ruckus.

"Shhh, Turbo, it's okay." Darius patted the dog's head.

"I'm going to shower." Melissa grabbed the towel from the night before off the floor.

"You showered last night."

"A lot has happened since then. This morning, I smell like your cologne and sex." She flicked the towel in his direction.

"Come here and let me see." He held his arms out for her.

"No way. If we're going away, I've got a lot to do. The last one in the kitchen cooks breakfast." She smiled and closed the bathroom door.

By the time she dressed and made her way downstairs, he was already at the stove. "I would have cooked for you. I always pay my debts and keep my promises." She came up behind him and wrapped her arms around his waist.

"I'm glad you remember your comment. Because you promised to come with me to Maui and I have my assistant making the arrangements. We're leaving first thing tomorrow morning."

She squeezed him tighter. He folded over the fluffy eggs, enclosing the melting cheese into a perfect omelet. "So you were serious. I thought that was just your sexual appetite talking."

He turned to face her. The way his eyes roamed over her body made her blush. The blaze of his pupils sparked a burn in the base of her soul. She wanted to pull him into the pulse of her heart so he'd know just how much she loved him.

"My love for you was talking. I meant every word. This is a fresh start for us and this time will be different. After this mini tour, I'm talking to my publicist to find opportunities to get us on every front page of every rag paper and news show she can think of. Maybe I'll even go on my favorite morning gossip show too." He nodded to the television just as Sunny Kincaid took the seat in front of the studio audience.

"Are you serious? You're sure you're ready to expose our private life?"

He slipped his hand around her waist and pulled her so close she could feel him inhale. "I'm sure." He held her gaze. "I should have done this from the beginning."

He bent just enough to plant a kiss on her lips before tilting the frying pan and allowing the omelet to slide onto the plate. Then, he repeated the process for the second egg.

"You don't mind if your name is mentioned on gossip shows across the world?"

"Not at all." He smiled.

After sitting, they discussed the logistics of their trip. Going to Maui in the middle of the semester would be the most decadent thing she'd done in years.

He shoved a mouthful of eggs into his mouth. After swallowing, he put his fork down.

"The two of us is all that matters. At least, until we start our family."

Melissa gagged on the coffee, spewing it across the table. She swallowed the liquid left in her mouth and wiped her lips. "Did I just hear you say the F word? Are you really my husband or has his avatar moved into his body and taken over?"

He picked up their empty plates and placed them in the sink. "Oh, you think I'm joking, huh? Well, just wait and see. When I get you in Maui, I plan to get so busy, you might not get to see the black sand beach."

A large hoot escaped from her throat. This was so much fun, the way it used to be, the way she remembered. If this was just a phase he was passing through, killing time until he took off for his next music tour, she didn't know how she would come out on the other side. The thought was too depressing to entertain for more than a few seconds. Darius was the man she loved. He couldn't hurt her again. Together they had made it over the burning sands. Rehashing the past would be a bad idea.

Darius held out his hand to help her up. He wrapped his arms around her. He rocked her slowly, nuzzling his chin in the center of her head. While humming a melody, his hand snaked into her shirt and cupped her right breast. She closed her eyes and allowed her body to sway with enjoyment. In the short space of twenty-four hours, she'd stepped into a fairy tale, where her every wish came true. Now, all she had to do was lock the door and refuse to ever leave.

As his hand moved to caress her other breast, she twisted just enough to kiss him. His soft, warm lips felt smooth and tasted like honey. While he concentrated on her nipples, she deepened the kiss, wanting to have all of him.

The steady rise of heat between her legs made it impossible to stay still.

"It's been a long time since we made love in the kitchen." His voice was husky.

She unsnapped his pants and reached for his hard shaft. "There's no time like the present."

"Floor or counter?" he asked.

"Floor." Without releasing him, she wiggled out of her shorts and panties. He pulled the shirt over her head and caught a breast in his mouth. His index finger stroked her with such tenderness she melted in his hand. She undressed him and ran her hand along his sleek body.

"God, I've missed you so much. Thank you for giving us another chance." He pulled her down on the heated floor, parted her legs and eased inside. The warmth of him as he entered her shattered the remaining doubt.

Chapter Ten

As the driver maneuvered the car away from the curb at the Kahului Airport, she appeared relaxed and happy. Convincing Melissa to make the trip was easy. Helping her get everything ready to leave was the challenge. Somehow, she'd managed it all.

He placed his hand on her thigh. "The scenery will get prettier once we get away from this area."

"I already think it's fantastic. And I love the idea that we'll have our own villa."

"We'll have more privacy. I think we deserve to be treated like royalty, so I hired a cook and a housekeeper too."

She leaned closer and kissed him. "Thank you. I always thought we'd be middle-aged before we found the time to come to Maui. This is a real treat. I just wish we could be here longer than a week."

"I promise to bring you back." He rubbed her knee.

"You've been making a lot of promises lately." She gave him an earnest glare.

"And I intend to keep every one of them. You're more than just special to me, you're everything to me and for the rest of my life, I intend to prove just how special you are."

Tears gathered in her eyes. She tried to hold them back by biting her lip.

"Don't cry. This is supposed to be fun, a new beginning for us. So while we're here, everything else stays behind. No more dredging up what used to be. Do we have a deal?"

She nodded. He wiped away the tears clinging to her lashes and rolling down her cheek. "If you don't stop crying, you're going to miss the beautiful scenery along Route 30." He pointed out the window. "Look, there's the ocean."

"It so hard to believe we've come so far. I didn't think it was possible." She glanced out the window. "Is that a public beach?"

"Yes, want to stop?"

For several moments, she stared without saying a word. Her eyes grew larger. "I've seen special places before, so why does this feel so superior to anything else? The water is so blue, the weather is perfect." She took a deep breath and pressed her hands to her chest. "Okay…okay, I need to slow down and just enjoy our time here. Let's go to the villa, I'm sure the view from there will be just as remarkable."

"I've only seen the pictures, but I think you're going to love it."

The drive along Route 30 kept her occupied until they reached Lahaina. After making a wrong turn, the driver found the hidden entrance to the small villa. They pulled into a circular drive lined with palm trees and pink lokelani. Melissa leaned forward to stare out the window. The one-story house appeared to be made of glass.

Melissa turned to him. "Darius, this is fabulous. I can't believe I almost turned down the opportunity to be here." She sounded like an awed child overwhelmed with the present she'd always wanted.

"Only the best for you from now on, baby." He kissed her cheek. Just as they stepped out of the car, the caretaker came out the front door.

"Mr. and Mrs. Bellamy, welcome. I'm Clint. We're all ready for you. Please leave the bags and head inside. I'll take care of everything."

"Thank you, Clint." Darius offered his hand to help Melissa out of the car.

Melissa pulled him into the cool interior of the house. She kicked off her sandals and wiggled her toes on the marble floor. "I think I've found the house I want to live in forever. Look at this place. It's indescribable."

Clint walked in behind them and cleared his throat. "I know you've just arrived and probably want to get settled, but the luau you wanted to attend starts in about an hour. You have just enough time to change and I'll drive you over." He wrung his hands. "I've placed your bags in the master bedroom." He pointed across the living space to a hall. "The master suite is on the left facing the ocean. Will anyone else be joining you this week?"

Darius pulled Melissa against his chest. "Nope, it's just us two. Just the way we want it. Let's just say we're on our honeymoon."

Clint bowed his head. "Very well, sir. I'll wait in the drive."

Darius reached for Melissa's hand and led her down the hall. "I think we have enough time to christen this joint before dinner," he whispered in her ear.

"If not, we'll make time," she replied with a wide grin.

Chapter Eleven

Melissa positioned her head against the car seat so she could see the scenery as they drove the short distance to the luau. Darius rested his hand on her thigh, just below the hem of her mini dress.

Everything was perfect. The thought seemed foreign to her. After the turmoil of the last two years, she believed Darius, the prodigal husband, had returned to their marriage. She was ready to run into his open arms, repair their relationship, and live the dream she'd imagined for them.

There was one nagging thought that wouldn't release her. Darius was known for his propensity to stand his ground until he got his way. To him, winning was everything and his singing career was the one thing driving him for the last two years. So, what was different now? Was he giving up something or was she? Would he resent her if he never saw his name in the credits of the silver screen?

"Are you happy, Darius?"

Before answering, he searched her face, as if she'd spoken in a different language. "Of course I am. Why do you ask?"

"Well, we've gone from point A to point B and I'm not sure what's different. Have we settled anything?" She put her hand on top of his and gave him a gentle squeeze.

"I needed to make some changes. I understand that. But just so we're on the same page, I don't care if my fans know we're married. I want you beside me. I'll wind up the tour just about the time you complete the school year and I want you there with me."

"You make it sound so simple and easy. Why did we agonize over it and almost let it tear us apart?"

She could see him searching for an answer, but he didn't respond.

She said, "I don't know. It wasn't that I minded standing beside you and not being identified as your wife, but you were always gone. Lately, I spent weeks, sometimes months, without seeing you. I don't think we can have a marriage if our main form of communication is a late night call between shows. We stopped making our marriage a priority. Once we started pretending we weren't married in public, we forgot to reinforce our vows at home." She was as guilty as he was. She'd allowed her resentment to chafe at their bond until there was hardly enough to hold them together.

"Now, we know better. Let's not make the same mistakes again." He kissed her forehead.

"I promise." She rubbed her hand along his arm.

"Give me a chance, you'll see."

She nodded.

He turned his upper body to face her. "So, let me ask you. Are you happy?"

Without hesitating, she responded, "In this moment, my feet aren't on the ground. I feel like my fairy godmother has turned the pumpkin into this Town Car and my sandals into crystal slippers and my husband into my prince. I'm a little afraid delving too deep might cause the magic to disappear."

He pressed his lips to hers.

The car slowed at the entrance of the hotel, where the luau was taking place. She cracked the window to allow the island music to drift into the quiet interior.

"Are you ready to have a good time?" Darius asked as the car pulled to a stop.

Clint opened the door and they slid out.

"I am. Let's do it."

An attendant appeared and escorted them to a table near the stage and just right of the long buffet.

They took their seats at the private table and she leaned against his shoulder. The hustle and bustle of the day had drained her energy and sitting for few moments felt relaxing. Having these days with Darius's undivided attention was like being tucked safely in a cocoon.

"This is nice." He swayed with the music.

The smell of roasted pig and grilled meat woke up her stomach and her mouth started to water. She turned to the table laden with food.

"I haven't eaten since we left home this morning. I'm starving. Can we eat now?" she asked Darius as she pushed away from the table, tipping over the folding chair.

He grabbed her chair before it hit the ground. "We have premium tickets. If you want to eat, then my baby eats."

He escorted her a short distance to the forming line, several heads turned in their direction. Melissa guessed some of the patrons recognized Darius but were much too well-mannered to charge him for pictures or autographs. For a few days, she didn't want to share her husband. She'd just gotten him back and wanted to relish the tenderness blossoming between them.

Over dinner, the ugly two years fell away. They could have been the starry-eyed twenty-year-olds on their honeymoon, unaware of all the pitfalls waiting to send them tumbling towards divorce.

Her head snapped up. She hadn't told Darius a thing about her trip to the lawyer. A small prickle of perspiration dotted her back as a sense of uneasiness claimed her. Every time she started to bring it up, she hesitated, not wanting to end the idyllic atmosphere surrounding them. They were having such a good time. She didn't want to taint it with the reality of how close they had actually come to the edge. Maybe in a few years, when they could think back to the rocky times and laugh about their stupidity, she would tell him about her trip to seek legal counsel about their marriage. For certain, she'd call the attorney when they returned home and ask him to burn the papers.

"Do you want something to drink?" Darius asked, bringing her thoughts back to the festivities.

"Yes, I want a pineapple drop. They're very popular here."

The intensity of Darius's stare caught her off guard. "Have I told you how lucky I am to be married to you?" He kissed her and walked away without waiting for a reply.

She kept her eyes on him as he maneuvered across the large lawn to the bar. The loose-fitting shirt did nothing to conceal his well-developed body. She returned her attention to her plate while contemplating all the wicked things she could do to him when they returned to their villa.

A tall man with dark shades slipped into Darius's seat.

"Excuse me, but—" she started.

"I'm not going to stay long. I happened to notice you from across the way. We used to work together, your first year at the university. Don't you remember me? Rob." He lifted his sunglasses to reveal his green eyes. But the slight bend in his nose and the blond ponytail couldn't be mistaken.

"Rob!" she squealed. "I can't believe I've run into someone I know this far from home. How are you?" She hugged him.

"I'm good. You look great." He held her hand while observing her body.

"Where are you now?" she asked.

"Believe it or not, I just completed my medical residency in North Carolina. This is a vacation of sorts for me. A celebration."

"Well, congratulations. I knew you'd do it." She hugged him again. "Where's Charlotte?" Melissa tried to peer around him.

"Unfortunately, my marriage didn't last. She hated my residency. I was never home and we drifted apart. She drifted right into the arms of someone else." His eyes clouded over, revealing no emotion.

"I'm sorry."

"Don't be. It happens. She's happier now and so am I. How about you?"

Darius interrupted their conversation by clearing his throat. He held a drink in each hand. Rob jumped up from the seat.

"Darius, this is Rob. We used to work together before he abandoned the young minds for medicine." Melissa made the uncomfortable introductions. Darius's lips formed a tight line. Was there a tiny, green twinkle of jealousy in his eye?

Darius placed the glasses on the table and reached for Rob's hand. "Nice to meet you, man. So, how long ago was this?"

"It's been—"

"About four years now. I can't believe I ran into her." Rob continued to smile without taking his eyes off he, as if he didn't notice the daggers Darius shot at him.

Two weeks ago, maybe Rob's attention would have been welcome, but now, his presence made her stomach bubble. A thin slice of tension surrounded the three of them.

"Hey, you're Darius Bello." Rob glanced at her. "I didn't know you were married to this Darius. You never said." He looked from Darius, then back to her.

"I try to keep a low profile at the University. There aren't many people who know." She shrugged.

"Your secret is safe with me." He grinned.

"Rob, it's so good to see you. Again, congratulations." She gripped his arm and took her seat.

"Okay. Good to see you too." Rob lingered for a moment before dodging diners with full plates as he walked away.

"So, what was that all about?" Darius asked when Rob was out of earshot.

"Nothing. Just a friend. I can't believe I came all the way here and ran into someone who knows me."

"The way he was gawking at you, it seemed like he knew you really well. From the way he was staring, I thought he could see through your dress."

"Are you a little bit jealous, Darius?" She gave his shoulder a playful bump. "Now, you know how I feel."

He lifted a brow but continued to frown.

She tipped her glass against his and took a sip. "Cheers."

Chapter Twelve

Darius swung his legs up on the recliner overlooking the quiet ocean. From the villa's patio the waves licking the shore were barely audible. A cool breeze blew in off the water. Melissa had a wool throw draped around her legs; only her feet peeked from under the white blanket. Even though her eyes were closed, she tapped her finger to the beat of an Usher song drifting out onto the terrace. Her soft, extraordinary features were enough to keep him mesmerized. He could stare at her for hours and never get enough.

"You've been very quiet since dinner." He picked up his drink from the table.

She opened her eyes and adjusted her position to face him. The sun had set hours ago, but the moon bounced a bright beam of light off the water and onto the veranda. "I think I had too much to eat tonight. My stomach is stuffed."

"The food was delicious." He emptied his glass. "Are you sure you don't want something to drink?"

"I don't want anything."

"Did you enjoy the hula show?"

"I've enjoyed everything about this trip. I needed this more than I knew." She stared out over the rail into the gathering darkness. A peaceful silence settled around them. "How about you come sit on this recliner with me?" She moved to the edge and patted the open space.

"Gladly." He set the empty glass down and sat beside her. "Am I allowed under this blanket with you?"

"Please." She lifted the edge of the covering and beckoned him in. As the throw settled over the two of them, she nuzzled closer to him, unbuckled his belt, and slipped her hand inside his pants. Her fingers eased around his member, drawing life and blood into the region.

"If I had known this was on your mind, I would have asked to sit with you earlier." He pushed her dress further up her thighs. Her flesh was warm and soft. She emitted a low moan as his hand inched up her leg. He wanted to find the sweet spot between her thighs, but the longer it took him to get there, the more she enjoyed the ride.

With his free hand, he pulled her close until their chests were pressed together. He kissed her forehead, then trailed kisses along her temple and her cheek before landing on her mouth. She parted her lips just enough to allow his tongue inside. Her mouth was warm and wet. Instead of rushing her as she urged him on, he continued tangoing with her tongue for several minutes before deepening the kiss.

Sharing Melissa with someone else had never entered his thoughts until tonight. Watching another man stare at her like a divine piece of chocolate had sent a cold chill down his spine. He'd taken her for granted, expecting she'd always be by his side, satisfying his wants and desires. But tonight, the woman who sat beside him at the luau was exquisite and desirable. And the whole world could see what he had been ignoring.

He pushed the spaghetti strap down her arm and ran his tongue along the column of her neck and over her shoulder. She released the buttons on his shirt and cool night air blew across his skin when she removed the garment. Her fingers kneaded his chest, stirring his sexual appetite. Lust bubbled up in his loins like a molten pot.

"Let's take off your dress," he whispered.

"Out here, on the patio?" she asked.

"Yes. Isn't your fantasy making love outside?"

She laughed softly. "Yes…but…"

"Shhh, and turn around." He stood to help her remove her dress and slide her thong down her thighs. He squeezed her firm legs as he made his way to her feet.

Under the moonlight, her body glowed. Before returning to the lounge, he gazed down on her lean frame, perfect in every aspect. Her full breasts heaved with each breath. He knelt beside the chair and wrapped his mouth around her perfect nipple while stroking the other with his hand. She drew closer to him, clawing at his back as if she couldn't control her passion. The blanket slipped off the chaise onto the floor.

Losing Melissa would tear his heart out of his chest, like a bulldozer digging a crater in the earth. This week he needed to prove to her he'd turned his life over. She was more crucial than his singing career, or the next album, or the Hollywood deal. She was vital to him, like oxygen.

He drew out her nipple and captured the other one. Melissa began to rotate her hips in a slow circular motion, each rotation heightened his need. He released her and kissed the valley between her breast, her stomach, and the thin strip of hair leading to the spot he sought. Pressing his tongue against her nub, he suppressed the explosion blooming inside of him. She spread her legs just enough to allow him entry while she tugged on his ears. The movement of her hips increased in speed as she tugged harder on his ears.

When her body went still and she tightened her hold on his head, he slowed the pressure and eased her across the edge of bliss. Her body quaked with tremors as if from an earthquake. She shouted his name loud enough to be heard on the other side of the house. She continued to repeat his name in a thick, heavy murmur. He kissed his way back up her body and quieted her moans when he pushed his tongue in her mouth.

"Ah, Darius, I love you so much," she said.

"I love you too, Melissa." He peered into her eyes waiting on her answer.

Without delay, she nodded. "Yes. Yes, I know."

He slipped inside her wet folds and allowed her to pull him down. He pushed deeper, wanting to seal them together, forging a bond that couldn't be broken by the trivial mishaps waiting to unravel them like before.

With his head tucked into the side of her neck, he captured the soft skin between his teeth. Careful not to hurt her, he tried to lavish his love on her as it filled him up and washed him up on the shore like the evening tide.

Chapter Thirteen

Melissa looked down at her sleeping husband. The peaceful expression on his face proved how much he'd needed this time away too. After an evening of sex on the patio and in the master suite, he'd slept through the night without a single snore.

She glanced at the clock. It was almost ten o'clock and the day invited her to join in. She thought he'd be awake by the time she showered and dressed, but he hadn't even changed positions.

"Darius, wake up and come running with me." She stretched her quadriceps. He opened one eye to peek at her.

"You've got to be kidding me, right? After last night, I'll need a few more hours." He tugged the sheet over his shoulder.

"Ah, come on. We can go running on the beach. How often do we get to do things together?" She pulled on her other leg.

"Tell you what, you get a head start. I'll catch up with you." He closed his eyes and turned on his side.

"Yeah, I bet," she called over her shoulder as she walked out of the room.

She made her way through the house. In the kitchen, the sound of opening and closing cabinets caught her attention.

"Mornin', ma'am. Are you ready for breakfast?" Clint asked while a woman she hadn't met cracked eggs against a bowl. "Carmelita will have breakfast ready in a few minutes."

"Carmelita, it's nice to meet you. But hold up on breakfast. Darius is still sound asleep and I'm going for a run. By the time I get back, maybe sleepy-head will be ready to eat." She set her sports watch. "Give me about forty-five minutes."

"Sure, no problem." Carmelita wiped her hands on the apron around her ample waist and put the bowl in the refrigerator.

"Clint, is there a coffee shop down the road?"

"Yes. It's a long way."

"I don't mind. After all I ate last night, I need a long run. If Darius asks where I am, let him know I'll be back shortly."

Clint nodded.

Outside, she cranked her neck left, then right. Instead of running on the beach, she turned in the opposite direction and headed toward the small strip mall they'd drove past on the way home from the luau.

The moment her feet hit the pavement, happiness filled her lungs. With each step, she shook away all the dogma collecting in the corners of her life. Thinking about Darius made her smile, the way it used to in the beginning. For so long, she had thought all their good times were behind them, now she knew better.

The crisp morning air fueled her for the first mile. Exhilaration for the new path she and Darius had found provided the energy for the second mile. By the time the coffee shop came into view, she was winded. She slowed her pace and came to a stop just outside the door. She placed her hands on her knees and tried to regulate her breathing. A wide wet spot stained the front of her sports bra.

"It's not you again? How do we keep running into each other like this?" Rob stood over her with a large cup in his hand.

She straightened and arched her back. "Get outta here. I don't believe this. Are you following me?" She managed to puff out the words while breathing hard.

"I'm not, but I could." He grinned.

"And like I told you before, it wouldn't do you any good." She placed her hands on her hips and nodded at his cup. "I see some things don't change. We both still need our coffee first thing in the morning, huh?"

He laughed. "You're right. Why don't you grab that table over there and I'll get you a coffee. Large with sugar and cream, right?"

"Yes, but now I'm on decaf," she said.

"Got it."

She plopped in the chair and grabbed a napkin from the small holder on the table. After wiping her forehead and neck, she took a deep breath. Two miles shouldn't have exhausted her. She depressed the chronograph on her watch and tracked her heart rate.

"Are you going to live?" Rob asked as he took the seat next to her and placed a cup on the table.

"You tell me, you're the doctor." She picked up the cup and blew into the small hole to cool the coffee. "I can't believe you're a doctor. You set your mind on something and you just did it. You must feel fantastic."

"I finally put me on top of the priority list. Instead of continuing to talk about what I wanted over and over again, I decided to do something to make my dream come true. How about you? Are you enjoying yourself at the university?"

She hesitated for a moment. Teaching was something she did. It didn't require much from her, but she didn't envision standing in front of a classroom for the rest of her life. Living in San Francisco was supposed to be for a short time. But moving back to the east coast never came up for discussion anymore. Darius traveled so much she felt like she lived in San Francisco alone, anchored on the west coast, miles away from her family.

"I don't know. I'm not buzzed about teaching the way I used to be."

"So, if you could do something else, what would it be?" He looked over his cup at her as he took a sip.

She stared at him, unable to answer his question. "I don't know. I used to think I wanted to be in PR. I pictured myself as a publicist. Hanging out with bigwigs in New York, being in the middle of something new and fascinating. But my heart has always been in art, drawing, and painting. In my spare time, I used to have an easel set up in our spare bedroom. Once, I even drew up a business plan to open a gallery."

"Then why don't you? What's stopping you?" She detected a hint of pity in his eyes.

"Darius is so busy and so connected on the west coast I just can't—"

"What does his career have to do with what you want? If you can't get to the east coast, then get started on the west coast. Think Hollywood. There are lots of people in Hollywood who restyle their homes yearly. They are always searching for something new and different. I think they would love to say they found the perfect piece at a local gallery," he encouraged her.

She laughed and sipped the hot coffee. He made it sound so easy, like she couldn't find her nose with her own fingertip. Was she being silly or was she afraid? "What if I throw open the door on my own business and no one shows up?"

He removed the lid on his cup and swirled the contents. "Well, you can sit on the sidelines and wonder, or you can jump into the game. I'll tell you what, jumping in is much more fun than just watching everyone else do their thing."

She agreed and took the first big gulp of her coffee. Rob patted her hand.

****

Darius picked up his pace, expecting to come up on Melissa or at least to see her in the distance. Sweat rolled down his brow. He jogged up to the coffee shop in time to see Rob reach for Melissa's hand.

He slowed his pace to a walk without taking his eyes off her. She gave Rob a smile that didn't reveal much, but she seemed happy. Maybe he was being silly, but how did the two of them end up here this morning? Melissa couldn't have planned this, could she? Coming to Maui had been his idea.

His heart pounded against his chest. He took a deep breath as he made his way to the table.

"Ahem."

Melissa's head snapped up to see him. "Darius…what are you doing here? When I left, you were still in bed. I thought you were sleeping in this morning."

"Obviously." He looked down at Rob's hand positioned on top of hers. She pulled her hand free. "We came here to spend some time together, so I decided to get up and try to catch you."

"Rob was just giving me some coaching advice."

Darius claimed the empty chair beside her, pushing his sweaty body closer to her so the two of them were on the same side of the table.

"Oh, like what?" Instead of giving her his attention, he glared across the table at Rob.

"About me continuing to teach or doing what I really want to do." She placed her hand on his arm and applied enough pressure to get him to look her way.

"You don't want to teach anymore? Why haven't you ever told me? You love it so much." Her confession felt like a punch instead of a declaration. Why hadn't she confided in him? He used to be the person she talked to about everything. When had she dropped his status below a casual friend?

Rob stood. "I really need to get back. You two take care." He seemed uneasy.

"Rob, you don't have to run off. If you have some good advice for Melissa, we'd like to hear it." The moment the spiteful words left his mouth, he wanted to draw them back. The uncomfortable feeling of seeing another man's hand on Melissa's wouldn't ease up. And if he had to fight to keep her, he would.

Rob's eyes darted to Melissa and back to him. "I better get going. You two enjoy your jog." He hurried down the street without a backward glance.

Melissa put her chin in the palm of her hand and glared at him. "What exactly is wrong with you, Darius?"

He ran his hand down his face. He deserved whatever she dished out. But he wouldn't be a fool or as forgiving as his father had been when he'd found out about his wife's indiscretion. "I don't know. Last night you were hugging him, today he's holding your hand. I don't know what to think."

"Well, you should know what *not* to think. I feel like I owe Rob an apology. He must think we're a bunch of kooks. I know I would. Do you think I set up a rendezvous with him here in Maui, right under your nose?"

He looked out beyond the parking lot to the traffic waiting at the light. A father on a bicycle with a baby seat attached on the back was waiting too. When the signal changed, he crossed the street while his son swung his feet. They seemed to enjoy the morning much more than him.

"You can ignore me, but one of these days you'll need to answer that question." She stood.

"I'm going back to the villa." She took off without waiting for him, leaving her coffee on the table.

His eyes were glued to her thighs as she sprinted down the street. When she disappeared around the corner, he pushed away from the table and stood. His calves were tightening. He bent at the waist and pressed his palms against the tips of his running shoes.

Of course, she was right. He'd planned the whole trip, she couldn't have set up a meeting, but logic didn't dispel the weight sitting on his chest. The heaviness warned him something bad was bound to happen. Life always had a surprise, and sometimes, they weren't good ones.

Several deep breaths did nothing to alleviate the uneasiness in his chest moving across his torso and into his legs. He shook his head, hoping the apprehension would move on to trouble someone else.

The jog back to the villa wasn't as satisfying as the run to the coffee shop. His limbs felt laden with dread. The last mile had him gasping for air until he finally slowed his pace. Melissa thought she was the only one marked by the dysfunction of her family, but the scars from his parents were just as deep and just as ugly.

He picked up speed and tried to draw more air into his aching lungs. At least the burn in his chest allowed him to focus on the external pain, the one he could control. Maybe his mother's little secret had warped him. After twenty years, letting it go might be the one act that could really set him free.

From the foot of the driveway, he saw Melissa lying on the floor of the veranda overlooking the ocean. With her hands behind her head, she stared at the clear blue sky. He made his way to her and flopped in the nearest chaise. She turned to acknowledge him without saying anything, then closed her eyes. He cleared his throat between deep gulps of air.

"Okay, my behavior was over the top. You would have reacted the same way." He rubbed his hands together.

She peeked at him again but said nothing.

"Aren't you going to talk to me?"

"I'll let you do the talking. What's going on?" She sat up straight, crossed her legs yoga style.

"I don't like Rob."

"That's not an explanation. What else you got?" She exhaled from her mouth. Her cool demeanor was unnerving. Melissa had a set of claws she only retracted when she was happy. From the glint in her eyes, she was a long way from happy.

"This is our vacation. I don't want anything intruding on us. I even told Dan not to call me."

"Darius, as much as you may want to, you can't control every situation. Rob isn't threatening our time together. How many times have I seen pictures of you in compromising situations or read a news story where an explanation was required? But I'm still here. If this is going to work you need to trust me too.

"But you know most of those articles about me are all made up."

"Some of it sounded pretty real to me. Don't believe for one moment I haven't had cause to wonder."

"It's the business, Melissa. How many times do I have to remind you?"

He jumped off the chair, turning his back to her. At the rail, he inhaled the smell of the ocean; the salt air stung his nostrils the same way her words stung. If he couldn't control his environment, then who would? No way could he live his life dangling from a string while someone else dictated his actions.

"Melissa, you know me well enough to know even though I can't control everything, I won't stop trying." He tightened his hold on the banister while turning just enough to see her face. He sighed. "I think we won't see Rob again. Let's just enjoy the rest of our week here. What do you say?"

For several moments, she looked at him without saying a word. Seagulls squawked while strutting along the beach. She stared at his face like she was searching for the right answer, but something kept her from closing the distance between them.

"You just have to trust me, Melissa."

"I want to, Darius. I used to." She stood up but remained a few feet away from him. "But you've got to trust me too. We can't let the baggage of our parents haunt us forever."

He opened his arms hoping she'd walk back into their marriage with a willing heart.

Without the wondrous amazement he wanted to see in her eyes, like when she'd said yes to his marriage proposal, she accepted his hand and the kiss to seal their deal. The nagging ache at the base of his neck reminded him to tread carefully. The minefield surrounding their marriage hadn't been disarmed by a mere kiss.

Chapter Fourteen

Melissa waited until the server disappeared behind the colorful partition before reaching for Darius's hand. Their truce had lasted all week. As the vacation drew to a close, the tension between them, along with the doubts, had eased out to sea with the tide. She didn't even want to remember what had started all the bickering and angst.

"I can't believe our week is up. The time went so fast," she said.

He stroked the tops of her fingers. "It seems like we just got here yesterday. But look at all the stuff we got to do. We even took the sunset cruise." He smiled.

"At least I managed to see the sun fall below the horizon before falling asleep," she laughed.

The waiter returned with a sparkling red wine. He made an elaborate show of popping the cork and filling their glasses. After taking their meal requests, he left them alone on the empty balcony.

"Are you sure you didn't keep me busy just to make sure we didn't run into Rob again?"

He almost smiled, even though his lips curled up, his face remained stoic. "You'd think by now I'd gotten past my old insecurities. But when I least expect them, they pop up again. Maybe that's the way it will always be."

"I'm not like your mother. You can trust me."

"Deep down inside, I know you're not. But I carried her secret for years, hoping my father wouldn't find out. Even though he never said it, I think he wonders why I never said anything to him about what was going on. So, under some circumstances, I'm always suspicious."

She leaned closer to him and squeezed his hand. "What happened between your parents was a long time ago. They seem to be doing fine. When your father found out, they worked through their problem. Now, their marriage is strong and they seem very happy."

"Sometimes my father gets in a mood and no one can understand his depression. I think the pain of my mother's adultery still dogs him."

"But he's happy, Darius. You believe he's alright, don't you?"

He nodded and refocused his attention on her instead of the silverware on the table. "I don't want to talk about my family. This evening is all about us."

"How long has it been since we've spent quality time together?" she asked, while trying to decipher the distant look hiding behind his eyes.

"Obviously, too long. But this week brought us closer together."

"How do we take what we're feeling back home with us?"

He reached beyond the table to place his hand over her heart and his other hand over his. "We have to carry the passion in here, Melissa." He thumped his chest. "If it's not in here, we're doomed."

She nodded agreement. The sincerity in his voice left no room for vacillating.
Finally, the commitment she wanted from him was spoken under the full moon in one of the most romantic places on earth. Her heart swelled with each beat.

"This trip was everything you promised. I even know how to snorkel now. I have the scratches on my ankles to prove it." She stuck out her leg to show him.

"I told you to watch out for the coral," he chuckled.

"I'll remember to follow your guidance the next time." She lifted her wine glass and tapped his.

"Why don't you come with me on tour? This doesn't have to end. Think about how much fun we can have. I want you beside me."

As much as he wanted to have her on the road, she couldn't. The university needed her back in the classroom. Besides, going from city to city and listening to screaming fans was no longer her idea of fun. That was his dream, not hers. In the quiet moments between their adventures, she was able to decide on two important things. She wanted to save her marriage and it was also time to find something to make her as happy as music made him. And it couldn't be clinging to him.

"You know I can't. But I think after this semester I might not go back to the classroom."

Darius sat up straight in his chair. "You were serious the other day?"

"Yes, I was. I've been thinking about my career a lot for several months. My parents loved teaching. I just kinda fell into it."

"What will you do? I can't imagine you sitting around the house all day."

"My sisters have found their passion. I think it's time I pursue mine."

"You're going to paint?" For the first time since they sat down to dinner, his eyes lit up, sparkling like sea glass.

She shrugged her shoulders. "I might. I'm thinking about it. And I may open an art gallery for up and coming artists. With my own place, I can help someone else and display my pieces too."

He nodded as if the thought had to be absorbed. "I like the idea. It's about time you got back to your canvas."

"I'm only thinking about the options. I haven't made up my mind yet."

"What brought on this change?"

She didn't dare tell him that all the talk about careers and passion had tilted her universe and knocked her off kilter. Her parents had always assumed she'd be a teacher, so, while growing up, it was easier to assume the position than it was to fight with them. But now everything was different; pleasing them was no longer required. If Rob could follow his dream for medical school, she could pick up her brushes and get serious.

"I've been thinking about this for months." She tried to sound nonchalant. "Right now it's only an idea. Stay tuned."

The server set their entrees in front of them. She caught a whiff of garlic and rosemary and the scent of his meat grilled in butter. Instead of diving into her favorite seared salmon, her stomach turned upside down.

"Are you okay? You look green." Darius stared at her.

She pushed the plate into the middle of the table to keep the smell away from her nose. "I just lost my appetite." She rubbed her stomach through the thin silk of her dress, hoping the wave of sickness wouldn't ruin their evening.

"Are you going to be okay or should we leave?" Darius put his fork down.

"No. We haven't eaten since breakfast. You have got to be hungry. Eat." She gestured to his sizzling plate as she tried to fight the throbbing feeling in her head.

"If you want to go back to the villa, I can have this wrapped to go. I really don't mind."

"Eat, sweetheart. I'll be fine."

Without waiting for more encouragement, he picked up his fork and cut into his ribeye steak. Watching him chew each medium rare hunk set her belly into another spin. When he finally put his fork down on the empty plate, she felt like she'd been released from food prison.

He paid the check. "We better get out of here before you start to hurl. If you get any paler, I might have to carry you back to the villa." He grabbed her hand.

****

The huge paddle fan in the middle of the master bedroom stirred up a nice breeze, but Darius cracked open the patio doors to allow air in the room. Melissa's color had returned the moment they left the restaurant and stepped out into the night air, so more ventilation had to be better.

"At least I waited until the last night of our stay before getting sick." She curled around him as he eased back into the bed.

"You had me worried for a while there."

"It was nothing, probably an allergic reaction. Whatever upset my stomach stopped as soon as we left the restaurant." She trailed her

140

finger down the center of his chest. "You know something else I noticed. You haven't been guzzling those energy drinks while we're here."

"You see, there's another reason why you should go on tour with me. I can take care of you and you can take care of me. I haven't had a desire or a need for one of those drinks in days." He pushed a ringlet of hair away from her face so he could stare into her deep, brown eyes.

She swatted his arm and laughed. "You mean I'll be taking care of you because when you're traveling you are just one big baby. I want no part of sitting around waiting on you hand and foot."

Hearing the light context in her voice eased his anxiety. They needed more time together to solidify their restart, but cancelling the shows was not an option. He pulled her closer, cupping her face with his hands as he kissed her warm mouth.

Trust. He had to trust they would be just fine.

He lowered his mouth to her lips. She tasted warm and sweet as she pressed the full length of her body against him. The smell of her cologne still lingered on her skin. She wrapped her legs around him, drawing them even closer. His erection pushed against her thigh, his need for her heavy in his loins. Being away from her for several weeks was unimaginable. He knew it was impossible to get enough of her to last him until he returned, but tonight, he wanted to try.

She released a moan as he massaged her breast.

"Did I hurt you?" he asked.

"A little."

"I'll be gentler," he responded. He took her nipple into his mouth and circled it tenderly with his tongue. He switched to the other breast and moved his hand down her body to the soft crease between her thighs. She opened her legs to allow his fingers to find her nub.

Melissa draped her arms around his neck and pushed her tongue inside his mouth. In rhythm, they explored each other until he felt unable to hold back the tide of pressure mounting in his body.

He pulled away from her to straddle her thighs. She seemed reluctant to release her hold on him.

"Baby, I want you now. I need you."

She nodded and untangled her legs as her hands gripped his shaft. She tightened her hold on him, almost causing him to explode with ecstasy.

"You better not do that," he warned. "I'm so close…"

"I am too."

He plunged into her like a burning man into water. The euphoria of being inside of her made him shudder. For several moments, he luxuriated in her warmth. This was the purest pleasure he knew. He could spend a lifetime in this position and still it wouldn't be enough. To love one woman with so much fervor had to have some downside, but for now, he pushed all negative thoughts from his mind and allowed his body to match her movement.

She drove her hips against him, demanding more. He thrust deeper into her, again and again until she began to claw at his back.

"Darius, now," she purred in his ear.

He climbed the mountain, and just as her frenzied movement stiffened, he plunged over the side. His body was transported to ecstasy.

Chapter Fifteen

Two days ago, they had been making hot, lusty love on the beach in Maui, and now, his driver was placing the last of his bags in the trunk of the car. She tried not to be sad, but she felt empty.

She stood in the doorway as Darius's limousine pulled away from the curb. With the darkened windows she couldn't see him, but she waved anyway. The cool morning air circled her bare ankles. She pulled her sweater tighter and shivered. The old familiar feeling of loneliness radiated through her veins as the car turned the corner.

She went back in the house. Without waiting another moment, she dug out the paperwork from the lawyer out of her purse and dialed his number.

"I'd like to speak with Mr. Daly, please. This is Melissa Conroy."

"He's in court this morning. Can I take a message?" The receptionist sounded just as frenzied now as she had when Melissa showed up in their office.

"Oh. Well, I stopped in to see him a few weeks ago about a divorce."

"Honey, he sees a lot of people about divorce. Let me pull your file."

Melissa heard papers shuffling and a hushed conversation, but she couldn't make out any words.

Turbo left his space near the fireplace and brushed against her leg. She scratched the top of his head.

"Conroy. I've got it. It says here you wanted a little time before signing. Are you ready now?" she asked in a clipped tone.

"No, actually we're not getting divorced. We made up. Maybe I was being hasty, but everything is fine now."

"Ha," the receptionist guffawed. "I'm not surprised. They always change their minds when they find out how much it's going to cost them or how much alimony they have to pay. We'll keep the papers on file for a year in case you change your mind."

"No. You don't need to do that. I'm certain," Melissa rushed. No matter what happened she wouldn't go back to Daly's offices. Maybe he should think about finding a new assistant, one who didn't drive business away.

"I'm following our policy," she snapped.

"Does your policy require me to remember to call you again, a year from now?"

"No," she said in the same clipped tone. "Not at all. If I don't hear anything more from you, we'll shred your documents."

Melissa sighed with relief. "Thanks." She eased the receiver back on the cradle. Maybe she should try to talk with Mr. Daly in person. The receptionist had had it in for her ever since she disrupted the discombobulated woman's schedule by showing up without an appointment.

The doorbell rang, startling her and setting Turbo into a fit of barking. She opened it without checking the peephole.

"Pam, what are you doing here?"

"Just because you and Darius have made up, are you kicking me to the curb?" Pam stepped in the house, dropped her drawstring bag on the floor and placed her hands on her hips.

"You'll always be my girl." Melissa hugged her friend.

Pam shrugged loose from the embrace. "You didn't even call me when you got back in town."

"Awww. Are you feeling abandoned?"

"Oh, shut up." Pam gave her a gentle shove. "You know I have abandonment issues. What's for breakfast? I'm hungry."

Melissa motioned her toward the kitchen. "Darius prepared some sausage and toast. My sinuses have been acting up, so I didn't eat. You can have mine."

Pam rinsed her hands in the sink and flopped into a chair at the kitchen island in front of the plate. "You sure you don't want this?" she asked as she picked up the link and bit it in half.

"Help yourself." Melissa pulled orange juice from the refrigerator and poured two glasses. As she set one in front of her friend, Pam gobbled up the first piece of toast and reached for the second. There were heavy bags under her eyes, and her dark roots needed a touch-up. "Pam, what's up with you? Do we need a day of TLC?"

Tears collected in Pam's eyes, but she continued to chew. "I tried to see Steve last night. He shut the door in my face."

Melissa held her. While she rubbed her shoulders, Pam shook with sobs.

"I was on the phone all night with my mother. I couldn't stop crying. Even though I tried to convince her I was going to be okay, she's adamant about coming out here."

"Maybe she should. She might be able to comfort you and help you move on. It's obvious what I'm doing isn't working," Melissa tried to reassure her.

"I just thought after a few months maybe his mood would have improved and he'd be ready to sit down and talk."

"I thought we agreed you were going to leave him alone, honey."

"I still love him, Melissa. How can he move on so fast? He had to be cheating on me."

"Don't do this, Pam." She held her at arm's length and tried to get her to focus. "Why don't we go get our nails done and get a massage? Maybe a day on the town will help you feel better."

Pam reached for a napkin on the counter and wiped her nose.

****

Darius called home. After four rings, the recorder came on. From the backseat of the town car he glanced at the digital clock display. Where could Melissa be this time of day? She'd sworn she needed to get caught up on paperwork and would be home all day.

After a few minutes, he redialed. Again, no answer. She didn't answer her cell, either. After the message prompt, he said, "Call me." He couldn't suppress the terse sound in his voice. Why wasn't she picking up anywhere? He shoved the phone back into his jacket. Seven hours and they were right back where they started. He tugged at the collar of his shirt. Distrust gnawed at him, and as much as he wanted to ignore the feeling, it was hard. Melissa was not like his mother, sneaking around with someone else while he was on the road. And Darius knew he could never be like his father and forgive her if she ever did.

"What's gotten into you? You're fidgeting like a prostitute in church. Don't tell me you're nervous about the concert?" Dan asked from his side of the car.

"It's nothing."

"Darius, talk to me, man. I'm here to listen to you."

"I'll be fine when I get on stage. I got this."
He slid closer to the door. "Are you sure the dancers
know their steps? I don't want another incident like
we had last time." He tried to take the edge out of
his voice.

"Gwendolyn decided to quit the group and
stay home with her baby. Her replacement is really
good. You can meet her when we get to the arena."

Traffic out of JFK International Airport was
congested. As the car inched toward downtown, he
kneaded his neck to keep the tension at bay.
Tomorrow, he needed all of his cylinders firing red-
hot. Before the press conference tonight, he'd try
her again.

Chapter Sixteen

Melissa unlocked the door to the house just as Pam's phone started to chirp. After a day of retail therapy, the dark circle under her eyes had lightened and the crying jags had stopped. Pam dropped her bags in the entrance to pull her cell from her purse.

"It's my mother. Should I answer it?" Pam asked.

Melissa placed her packages in the nearest chair. "Girl, I'm still on a shopping high. Let me stay there a little longer. I'll go get us something to drink." Melissa left Pam standing in the foyer.

In the kitchen, she glanced at the phone. The red message light was blinking. It was probably Darius telling her he'd arrived in New York. She glanced at the clock on the microwave. If she could get Pam settled, she might be able to reach him tonight.

She unzipped her boots and kicked them into the corner. Turbo stuck his nose into one of them. "Dog, leave my shoes alone. Don't even think about it." She pulled a Milk Bone from the box under the sink and placed it in his mouth. He stretched out on the floor with the treat between his paws and began gnawing on the end.

After extracting her cell phone from her purse, she retrieved the voice mail from Darius.

"Call me." His voice was like a cold blast freezing her in place. The warmth she expected to hear in his message was missing. The two-word command echoed in her head while her stomach battled to right itself. She set the phone on the table face down and opened the refrigerator.

"What do you want to drink?" she yelled to Pam while examining the icebox and trying to push his voice out of her head.

Pam came into the kitchen. "Just give me water. After such a big dinner, I can't drink another thing," "How is your mother?" Melissa placed a bottle of water on the counter and poured herself a glass of milk.

"Since I'm not crying and sound coherent, she's less likely to jump on a plane to fly out here to rescue me. I told her we spent the day together, so I think I appeased her." Pam opened the bottle and took a long swallow. "I think I've come to a conclusion today. I'm moving back to the east coast. Other than you and Darius, I have nothing here. The two of you have each other, so I'm going back home to find my own love." Even though the words were upbeat, there was no happiness in her voice.

"Hopefully, in time you will convince yourself you're doing the right thing," Melissa said before propping her elbow on the island. She didn't want to think about having her best friend so far away. "How soon do you think you'll leave?"

"In a few weeks, maybe a month. The way I figure, the sooner the better. The more miles between me and Steve, the sooner I'll get over him." She stood. "I should get out of here. I've got a pile of tissues I need to put in the trash and a bottle of wine chillin' in the fridge. Besides, the last thing I want to hear is lovey-dovey talk between you and Darius."

"He's out of town for a few weeks. And based on the message he left for me, there may not be a whole lot of loving conversation. Why don't you stay here tonight? We can have girls' night."

"On a Friday night? Just the sound of that is downright pitiful. Thanks, but no thanks. I'd rather go home and watch re-runs of Friends. No offense."

Melissa laughed. "None taken."

In the foyer, Pam grabbed her bags and planted a kiss on Melissa's cheek.

"Call me in the morning," Melissa said to her friend as she ran down the steps. "I mean it, Pam. If I don't hear from you by ten, I'm coming over."

"I'm not suicidal, Melissa. I'm just alone." She waved.

Melissa closed and locked the door. Back in the kitchen, she picked up her phone and dialed Darius. It was one o'clock on the east coast. His concert might be drawing to a close. She tapped her fingers against the glass table as she listened to the rings.

"Hey," she said when he picked up. "I really didn't think I'd get you. How was the show?"

"Where have you been? I called on both phones as soon as we landed and you didn't pick up either one." His accusatory tone bumped her temperature up several degrees. Where was the sweet, considerate man she'd relaxed with on the beach just a few days ago? Were they bound to be at odds whenever they were apart? Where was the trust that should have sheltered their love?

"I shouldn't have to explain myself. But if it makes you feel any better, Pam stopped by as soon as you left. You know what she's going through. She was in a mood, so I spent the day trying to cheer her up. We got massages, did some shopping, and stopped for dinner." The words rushed out. Having to justify her behavior angered her even more. "I'm sorry. I didn't know I needed your permission to have a life while you were enjoying yours."

He paused for several moments. "I'm sorry, Melissa. I just wanted to hear your voice when I got here, and then, when I couldn't reach you…I'm really sorry, sweetheart. I'm so glad you called me. I miss you so much."

As his tone softened, so did her mood.

"How is Pam?" he asked.

"Not so good. She's moving back to Philly. Maybe it's for the best. But I miss her already." She paused. "So, how was the show?"

His voice gained animation as he detailed his performance. His excitement fueled her adrenaline. Unable to stand still, she strolled around the kitchen while he recanted every component of his day. As he talked, the emotion in his voice drew her closer to him, recapturing the happiness she'd gotten used to in Maui.

"How ya been feeling? Any better?" he asked.

The affection in his tone made her smile. "No headaches, but my stomach is still funky. As a matter of fact, I'm heading to bed soon." She glanced at the untouched glass of milk on the counter.

"Are you going to find out what's the matter, or do I need to drag you to the doctor?"

"If I'm not better soon, I'll make an appointment next week. I promise."

"Okay, now, tell me what you're wearing." His voice slipped into a seductive whisper. She glanced down at her skinny jeans and oversized sweater.

"Absolutely nothing. As a matter of fact, I'm standing in the kitchen in my birthday suit, just waiting for you to ask me."

He laughed. "You're fully dressed, aren't you?"

"I am. How about you; what are you wearing?"

"Baby, I'm in boxers. Nothing but boxers. And I'm not lying. But no matter what you have on, I have a real good image of what my sexy wife looks like when she's really naked. If I close my eyes, I can almost believe I'm touching your luscious, perky breasts. I'm going to fall asleep with that image plastered on my brain. I'll call you in the morning. Melissa, I love you."

"I love you too. And I can see right through those boxer shorts."

Darius broke into a full laugh. She couldn't help but join in.

"I'll sleep on your pillow tonight just to be closer to you." She clicked off. The moment she put the phone down, her heart called out to him. She felt connected to him in a way that transcended logic. Her heart would forgive him of anything.

After gathering her bags from the entry hall, she made her way to the second floor. With a thud, she dropped the packages in the middle of the bedroom and undressed. "Turbo, stay away from my stuff." She tapped the bed. The dog jumped up next to her and immediately dropped his head on his paws. "I guess I'll let you keep me company tonight."

In the empty house, the quiet bounced off
the walls and heightened the feeling of loneliness.

156

Chapter Seventeen

Darius stretched his hands toward the ceiling to loosen the kinks from his back. Without an energy drink, it was hard to get going in the morning. His system needed refueling. He closed the door behind the room service attendant and surveyed the cart. Eggs, toast, juice, and coffee would have to suffice. He climbed on the bed, balanced the tray on his lap, and turned on the television. After propping the pillows up, he flipped through the channels until he found *the Sunny Kincaid Show*.

With a fork in one hand and his cell phone in the other, he called Melissa.

"Wake up, sweetie," he said as soon as she picked up the phone.

She grunted something he couldn't make out. He smiled. She wasn't a morning person.

"Come on, Melissa. It's Friday. You have an eight o'clock class, which means it's time for you to get out of bed and start moving."

"Darius, what time is it?" Her voice sounded like she was gargling with marbles.

"Ten here in New York, for you it's six. Which means, if you don't get up now, there is no way you're going to make the drive across town in time for your class at eight." He chuckled. They had the same discussion every week, even when he was at home.

"Why are you so happy this morning?"

"Because I dreamt about you all night. Girl, the things you did to me should be illegal."

"Oh, yeah. Well, in my dream, you were pretty naughty too. So, just imagine what we'll do to each other when we get together."

"I can't wait, baby." He laughed. "How's my dog? Are you taking good care of him?"

"Yes, I am. He's my dog now. As a matter of fact, he slept on your side of the bed."

"I've only been gone for one night and you've replaced me."

"Only until you come home. Then you know you'll be my number one."

"I'll bet you say the same thing to all your men," he teased. "Guess who came to my show last night?"

"Let me see…thousands of screaming girls waving their panties."

"Very funny. Actually, Sunny Kincaid was seated near the front row with her daughter. She did a brief interview with me after the show."

"Why didn't you tell me about your adventures last night?"

"It slipped my mind. The interview wasn't prearranged or formal, just an impromptu kind-of-thing."

She laughed. "Darius, you are probably the only famous person who goes gaga over someone who is as popular as yourself. You seem surprised to see her at your show."

"I'm not so excited that she was there, but if she'll talk about my performance on her show this morning, I'll get some free advertising. And I like free."

"I'm sure she will. I'll even tape her show for you. So when you get home you can watch it over and over again."

"Oh, you've got lots of jokes, don't you? I know you think it's silly, but grant me this one indulgence."

"Honey, you're fine. I like teasing you. Look, I need to get moving. I think Turbo needs to go outside and I better get dressed. Where is your concert tonight?"

"In Washington. I'll call you after the show. There are three days before the next gig, so I'm flying home right after the show. I've got a charter, so I should be there by morning."

"You're kidding me, right?"

"No. I miss you. I figure I can come home, get enough good loving to carry me for the next couple of concerts."

She hesitated for a moment. "Is something wrong, Darius?"

"Nothing a little time with you won't cure. I'll have a bottle of wine chilling for you when you walk in from class."

"I'm looking forward to it. And thanks for waking me up. I can't think of any better way to start my day." She blew him a kiss before hanging up the phone.

He nestled back against the pillow, pulled the serving tray closer, and sipped on his orange juice. Sunny glided across the set in her five-inch heels and sat on her cushion sofa. She started dishing out the latest industry gossip by focusing on the grand opening of a new celebrity restaurant. Darius buttered toast, hoping she'd mention the concert. An endorsement improved his odds of getting the movie score. Each step put him closer to his dream. He couldn't wait to tell his father some good news.

"How many of you went to the Dark Drizzle concert last night at the Garden? Did you see that fine-looking Darius B? Real nice eye-candy, and his voice?" She nodded and emphasized her words. He tried not to smile. *"He could sing to me all night long and I'd tell my husband he'd just have to get used to it. You know, I talked with him briefly after the show. He was very friendly. I wonder if he's dating anyone we know? Someone as good-looking as him has got to be attached, doesn't he? But he must keep it hush, hush. I haven't seen any notable*

pictures of him with anyone lately. Why don't you Sunny fans find out for me and let me know. Send it to me on Twitter or Facebook. And you know I love pictures. " She nodded again.

Darius wanted a comment about the concert, not about his appearance or an investigation into his love life. And if one of her fans found out about Melissa, then all the better. The whole world could know. They'll know anyway in just a few months when she shows up on his arm at the next awards ceremony.

His phone chirped with Dan's ring.

"Yeah, Dan, I heard it," he said.

"I knew you'd be watching. Isn't it great she mentioned the show?"

"Why are you so excited? You didn't do anything to get the promo. It was pure luck she was in the audience. She just brought her daughter to the show. Now, get me some free TV footage for the DC show, then I'll give you a pat on the back."

"You're a tough customer, Darius."

"It's not personal; it's just business. What time is the car picking me up?"

"Noon. I'll knock when they get here."

"Hey, Dan, for the publicity, don't do anything Melissa won't approve of. I'm not signing on for any nonsense."

"Yeah, but—"

"Nope, not open for discussion." He ended the call.

Chapter Eighteen

Darius unlocked the door to the house. Turbo charged at him with so much enthusiasm he had to back up.

"Hey, boy." He scratched the dog on his chin. "She lets you run free in the house now? This must mean she's locked up all her shoes." He followed the wagging tail into the living room and dropped his bag.

This visit home wasn't just about seeing Melissa. As much as he hated to admit it, he wanted to check in on her too. Make sure everything between them was as good as he'd imagined. The thought made him uneasy, but he was a realist. Every night some woman tried to get into his room or behind the stage, and if he was half-willing, she'd spread her legs for him.

He roamed through the rooms of the house. Everything was in order. Melissa would be home in less than an hour. He picked up the phone in the kitchen and ordered dinner from their favorite Italian restaurant. Afterwards, he set the small table on the porch and lit the hurricane lamps Melissa used for decoration.

His phone rang. He pulled it from the pocket of his jeans and checked the display. When he saw his father's number, he answered the call.

"Dad, how are you?"

"Son, where are you? I need to talk with you." His father's voice sounded strained.

Darius dropped into the nearest chair. "What's wrong?"

"She left me. I came home from a fishing trip and all her things are gone. She just cleared out, all gone."

"Mom?"

"Yeah." His father choked out a sob and cleared his throat. "I was half-expecting it. Lately, she was so quiet and withdrawn. Maybe this is the best thing for both of us. For too many years, we've been trying. I'm tired of trying, son."

Darius pulled his free hand down his face. "Did she say anything? Did she leave a note?"

"There's a note. But it doesn't make me feel any better. She says she doesn't want anything but her freedom. I wasn't keeping her locked down. She could have left anytime she wanted. She should have left twenty years ago when she…."

The line was quiet for several moments.

"Dad, are you still there?"

"I shouldn't have called you, but you are the only person who knows what we've been going through. And I needed to talk to someone."

"I flew home this morning or I'd jump in the car and come to New York."

"No. I don't want you to come home. I don't need rescuing. I just thought you should know.

We'll get together in the fall, just the way we planned."

"Are you sure?"

"Positive." His voice sounded stronger now. He asked about Melissa and the tour just like nothing of importance had happened, then he hung up.

Darius stared at the grout lines in the tiled kitchen floor without moving. He didn't want to take sides, but the acrimony he felt for his mother blossomed again.

He stared at the phone a long time before dialing her number. He wasn't even sure what he planned to say. She picked up on the first ring.

"You've talked to your father, haven't you?" she asked.

"Why, Mom? How could you hurt him like this again?" He knew he had no right to talk to her like a peer. But the boiling rage in his gut consumed him.

"Listen here, Darius. You might not like what's going on between your father and me, but don't think you can be disrespectful. You don't know everything, and I've tried to keep our business private. This is between me and your father. Our marriage was over a long time ago, but we kept trying to resurrect those ashes and it was just too exhausting. You don't need to know everything and I'm not telling you any more.

You're grown now. You've got Melissa and you guys are happy. I want to be happy too."

"But--"

"No, Darius. There are no buts. When you're done with this tour, we'll spend some time together. Not to talk about me and your father, but just to talk. Okay?"

He swallowed all the things he wanted to say. "Yeah, okay," he murmured.

Melissa came home and found him still seated in the kitchen.

"I thought you'd be happy to see me and rush to the door like Turbo." She kissed his forehead before moving to his lips. He parted his lips and accepted her tongue. More than anything he wanted to put his parents' problems out of his head, but they recycled on a constant loop.

The sweet taste of Melissa's mouth was enough to push away the disappointing conversation with his parents for a while. He lifted her in his arms and sunk his tongue deeper into her mouth. Allowing her to fill all the emptiness lingering in him. He released her so her feet touched the floor. All he wanted was to pretend life was good and perfect for a few moments. What he and Melissa had was more loving and caring than anything his parents ever shared. The urge to claim Melissa and demonstrate the depth of his feelings for her overwhelmed him like nothing else had in years.

"I've missed you so much," he whispered as he fumbled with the buttons on her shirt. "I can't decide if I want to take you here in the kitchen or upstairs in the bedroom."

"Mmm." Her throaty response heightened his lust. He pushed her skirt up and ran his hand along her smooth thighs. She buried her chin in the curve of his neck, breathing heavy.

"We'll start here and work our way upstairs." He helped her wiggle out of her tiny panties and dropped them on the floor. While she undid his belt buckle and zipper, he eased his finger between her moistened folds. The sound of her pleasure echoed in the room, drowning out the noise in his head.

He burrowed under her shirt and grasped her breast.

"Ouch."

"Sorry, baby." He reduced the pressure on her nipple and removed her shirt. He ran his tongue over the perky tip. The scruff of his unshaven chin brushed her skin, leaving red marks as he moved from one to the other.

He pulled away from her long enough to remove his clothing. She cradled his rod in the palm of her hand, pulling back and forth until he was ready to burst.

He bent her over the kitchen table and entered her. With his hands gripping her narrow hips, he eased in and out, careful to manage his hunger for her. Her response loosened the ache swelling in his heart. They were different. Their love was stronger. There were no hidden agenda's or secrets waiting to rip them apart.

Melissa pushed her butt higher, making his access easier. Her body stiffened.

"Darius, now," she demanded as she slammed against him.

He obeyed, holding her steady while he climbed to ecstasy. As soon as he caught his breath, he lifted her into his arms and made his way upstairs.

"I thought you were only kidding about making love in both places."

"I'll make love to you in ten places. You just name them."

****

Melissa threw her leg over Darius's and tried to catch her breath. Last night, he released her just long enough to eat the delicious dinner he'd ordered before taking her again and again. Tonight, he seemed insatiable. Her skin felt like it had been rubbed raw in places, but every moment was enjoyable.

She walked her fingers up his chest, feeling every muscle as she inched toward his Adam's apple. "I've eaten breakfast in bed, but never dinner. What a nice change."

"I think we were both too sore to eat downstairs." He wrapped his arm around her shoulder. "I missed you, alright?"

"We missed each other. But I wasn't expecting you to jump my bones as soon as I walked in the door."

"I only wanted to be with you. Besides, you stuck your tongue in my mouth. I had to give you my best. I want you to know what you're missing so you'll want me even more when I come home."

"I always miss you when you're gone for more than a day. I've told you the same thing so many times, I feel like if I never said it again, you'd already know."

"You could tell me the same thing every day and I'd need to hear you say it once more."

"You are about as tight as a girdle. There was a little anger in your lovemaking too. Are you still upset you couldn't reach me when you landed in New York? What's bothering you?" She sat up and moved behind him to massage his shoulders.

He told her about the call from his father and his call to his mother. He sounded stoic, but she knew him well enough to know the news had almost ripped him apart.

"Is your father okay?"

"He says he will be. But he didn't convince me."

"How did your mother sound?"

"She's always just fine. Nothing shakes the Ice Queen." His shoulders tensed.

"Maybe you aren't being fair. Nobody knows what goes on in a relationship, so nobody can judge what's right for other people."

"You always take her side. She's wrong, Melissa. You should have heard how hurt my father sounded." He shrugged away from her.

"Maybe she was hurting too. Should she stay married even if she's unhappy? Living an unfulfilled life wouldn't be fair to her." She tugged on his arm to get his attention. "Darius, you've let your parents' relationship color our interaction. Baby, you've got to stop visiting the bad things that happened to your parents on us. We aren't your parents. Our marriage is different."

He faced her. "Let's not talk about them anymore. I'm home for two days, and I've got an amazing weekend planned for us." The stare he gave her was clouded with more emotion than what registered in his voice.

He pulled her down on the bed and gave her a tender kiss. She accepted his tongue, even though the shadow from his parents' announcement still hung over them.

Chapter Nineteen

Melissa spotted Pam ensconced in a booth to the right of the hostess stand. She pushed her bag onto the leather-covered bench and sidled in next to it. "I'm sorry I'm late. I got wrapped up talking with a realtor talking about a storefront I saw that might be perfect for a gallery."

"No worries, I just got here. My drink hasn't even arrived yet." Pam pushed her hair behind her ear. "Did you and Darius enjoy your weekend at the Bed and Breakfast?"

"Yes and no. We had a nice time, but he was preoccupied with his parents' stuff. He tried to pretend, but I could tell he was thinking about them."

"At least he tried," Pam said. "I'd give a million dollars if Steve had been half as committed as Darius."

"You don't have a million dollars." Melissa laughed.

"I'd borrow it from you."

The waiter arrived to take Melissa's drink order.

"You're really going to do the gallery thing, huh?"

"Yes, I am. Since I've finally made the decision, I feel like a free bird." She threw her arms in the air. "I might teach another semester until I've got all the details worked out, but I'm excited."

Pam rested her chin in the palm of her hand and stared at the ketchup bottle positioned in the middle of the table. "Pretty soon I'm going to find my way too. I think as soon as I get away from all the reminders around here, I'll be able to put my life back together." She spoke without breaking eye contact with the condiments.

The hurt in her eyes was hard to accept. Melissa tried to manage the excitement bubbling inside. She wanted to run through all the details about the gallery and the artists she'd talked to, but the hollowed out shell of what used to be her best friend needed her attention.

"I'm going with you to Philly. To help you find a place," Melissa offered, hoping to provide some assurance.

"How are you going to leave your classes? You've got to work."

Melissa dismissed the comment by waving her hand. "I only plan to be at the university one more semester anyway. What are they going to do, deny me tenure?"

"I love the idea." Pam's eyes filled with tears. "I don't know what I'm going to do without you."

"I'll always be here for you." Melissa released her hand and picked up the menu. "Let's order some lunch. I haven't eaten much today and I'm starving."

Melissa signaled the server and they placed their order.

By the time they finished eating and walked out of the restaurant, Pam was back to her old self again. Her laughter came easily.

"You know what we need to do?"

"No, what?"

"We need to spend a day in Napa. I want to make sure I have a nice supply of all my favorite wines to take to Philly. I get cranky without my favorite beverage. Plus, we can have a fun weekend. Let's invite Asa and Dakota too." The giddy tone to her voice sounded like the vivacious Pam she knew.

"I love the idea. Set it up, I'm there."

After returning from lunch with Pam, Melissa flopped into the chair behind her desk. With her last class of the day over, all she needed to do was complete the mid-term exam questions and then she'd call it a day. At four in the afternoon, she was ready to go home and make some calls to some more artists, complete the business plan and sketches. Working well into the night was starting to catch up to her.

Sleeping with Darius on the road was like going to bed with a band of unruly distractions, each demanding a time in the spotlight. He'd only been gone a week and already it seemed like months. Talking two and three times a day just wasn't the same as having him at home.

Melissa tried to stifle a yawn.

"Wake up, sleepy head." A familiar voice interrupted her with her mouth wide open.

Melissa snapped her lips together and looked at the entrance to her office.

"Rob, what are you doing here?" She jumped out of the chair. He was dressed in jeans and a button-down white shirt, which accentuated his dark tan. With his dark hair and eyes, he could almost pass for 'a brother'.

"I had some business to finish up here at the university and I wanted to see some of my colleagues before I leave town. So, you know I had to stop by and see you."

"Leaving town? Where are you going?" She took a step closer to him. "Come on in and take a seat. Just excuse the clutter. You know what it's like in the middle of the semester." She pushed papers aside to make the desk more presentable.

"How about you walk with me down to the Coffee Shack? You look like you could use a change of scenery and I need to walk." Rob rubbed his hands together.

"What a good idea. I might as well call it a day. I was falling asleep. A walk will rejuvenate me." She grabbed her purse and briefcase. He waited while she locked the door.

The campus was nearly deserted. A few students mingled near the quadrangle, but she didn't recognize any of them. Melissa picked up her pace when a stiff breeze blew between the buildings.

"I don't think I'll ever get used to how cold it is in San Francisco in the spring," she said.

"Yes, you will. Give yourself a few more years."

They managed to find a small table in the back of the coffee shop. Melissa rushed to grab chairs relinquished by two women, each with a baby stroller.

"What are you doing on campus?" Melissa asked as soon as they were seated.

"Since my divorce is final, I needed to change my beneficiary statement and distributions on file. I didn't accumulate much during my short time at the school, but you know I'm a stickler for details. Also, I felt really bad about what happened in Maui and I wanted to apologize. I didn't mean to cause you and Darius any trouble."

She blew into her cup before taking a sip. "You didn't need to come down here just to apologize. Darius was just a little off. We've been going through a rough patch, and I'm sorry you got caught in the middle of our mess. Darius didn't mean to take his frustration out on you."

"I feel like I put you in an impossible position."

She waved her hand. "Nothing I couldn't handle." She reached across the table and squeezed his palm, hoping to reassure him.

He took a deep breath. "Good." He tasted his coffee. "I also wanted to tell you I'm moving to Baltimore. I'm doing my residency at John Hopkins."

"You're kidding me, right?"

He shook his head and grinned. "Nope. I'm dead serious. Since I'm making the career switch, I decided to go all out. The change of pace will do me good." He took another sip. "How about you? Have you made any decisions regarding your career? The last time we talked you were in a quandary."

"As a matter of fact, I have. After a lot of thinking and soul-searching, I've decided I'm going to start painting again, and I'm opening a gallery. I want to display new and upcoming artists along with some of my own pieces. I think I've even identified a location." She knew she sounded like an excited child. But every time she talked about the idea, the reality became more concrete. Her life had purpose now, and she didn't have to worry about living Darius's dream. For the first time in a long time, she felt equal to him in some way. She wasn't just living off him. They were both following their creative passions. And it had nothing to do with how much money he had or how little she made. Her chest filled with joy. She couldn't wait to share this new life with him.

"Great, Melissa. Your eyes are sparkling. Which means you're doing the right thing," he said.

"I think so."

He put his cup on the table and stood. "I better get going. I'm catching the red-eye out tonight and I have a few more loose ends to tidy up."

Melissa stood and embraced him. Another friend was abandoning her. With Darius touring and Pam moving away, who would she pal-around with? She pushed those thoughts aside. Somehow, she'd manage. Life would be so busy when the gallery opened, she wouldn't have much time for socializing, anyway. "Take care of yourself, Rob."

"If you're ever in Baltimore, give me a call."

She kissed his cheek. "Count on it." She waved as he made his way to the exit.

Chapter Twenty

Darius glanced at the clock on the side of the hotel bed. From the stream of sunlight filtering into the living area of his suite, it promised to be a beautiful day. So far, the tour hadn't produced any surprises. Dan deserved a pat on the back for planning so well. The routine of being on the road fueled his creative juices. Five songs for his next album were done, and the collaboration with Son of Summer was inked.

He reached for the phone and dialed Melissa. The next best thing to having her in the bed beside him in the morning was talking to her early, before he started his day.

She picked up on the first ring. "Good morning, Darius." Her voice sounded heavy with sleep but happy.

"How did you know it was me?"

She laughed. The soft chuckled only made him miss her more. "Nobody else calls this early. Besides, you call every day at the same time."

"I booked my flight. I should be there next Wednesday by the time you get home from school."

"Umm. I can't wait. Even though you've only been gone a few weeks, it feels like three months. What city are you in tonight? I've lost track."

"Atlanta. We're working our way down the east coast, then back up. After a short break, we'll finish in Philadelphia. But I don't want to talk about the tour. Tell me what's happening with the gallery.

"If everything stays on track, I should sign the lease later this month. It has an option for purchase, so the deal is even sweeter. I have talked with Vincent Michaels and he has agreed to show his work at my opening. Isn't that great? Everyone's been trying to get him, but he likes the idea of helping a local artist." The enthusiasm in her voice made him smile.

"You sound like you are about to burst with joy."

"I am. You and I are doing great, the gallery is coming along. What more could I want? If I don't get up and start my day, I'm going to be in trouble. But come May, all of this will be history," she said. "Besides, isn't Sunny Kincaid getting ready to air? I know you don't want to miss it."

"You're more important than any show, and don't ever forget that. I've got a surprise planned for you when I get home."

"Can't wait. You know I love surprises."

"Why don't you meet me in Philly for the show? We can have a celebration."

She hesitated. "I don't think I can. I'm moving full-steam ahead with gallery stuff. I think I can have it opened in a few months and I don't want to jeopardize the start up. You understand, don't you?"

He hid his disappointment as she blew a kiss before disconnecting the call.

The gallery wasn't even opened yet and already she was changing. Putting him second. He reached for the television remote. With three long days at home, they would have plenty of time to organize their schedules. A trip to her favorite bed & breakfast, the one she loved in the hill country, was already reserved. They would have the whole place to themselves.

The television picture came into full view just as Sunny positioned herself on the plush sofa. Her bright yellow dress was a stark contrast against the purple velour. She smiled at the studio audience and pumped her right fist into the air.

Darius climbed out of bed and made his way to the stocked mini bar. Instead of the 5-Hour Energy, he removed a bottle of water. Melissa would appreciate the healthier choice.

"Boy, do I have new news for you today. We'll discuss what's going on with my favorite reality show, Beverly Hills Madams. Did you all see the cat fight last night? But the biggest scoop is the upcoming divorce of Darius B. I didn't even know he was married. Stay tuned and we'll be discussing all that and a whole lot more after the commercial break."

Darius rushed back to the bedroom to stare at the television. He shook his head to clear away the sleep still clogging his ears. "What the…" he turned the volume up on the set and moved to the foot of the bed to wait for the show to come back on.

A series of commercials glued him to the flat screen. With each advertisement, his heart slapped against his chest.

He pulled his hand down his face. Maybe he'd misunderstood. After so many nights of loud music pounding in his ears, he couldn't be sure. Was this one of Dan's stunts? Maybe the time had come to break their contract. The antics were becoming ridiculous.

When the show returned, Sunny spent a lot of time talking about what the celebrities wore to a gala, and some reality show about women who were trying to become famous.

"Okay, everyone. This is hot new news. A few days ago I asked my viewers to find out if Darius B had a girlfriend. Well." She smacked her lips. *"Thanks to your help we found out he's married. And, just a month ago, his wife filed for divorce."* She leaned closer to the camera and dropped her voice to a whisper. *"Remember I told you all I was at his show a few weeks back? Well, it looks like while he is on the road, she ran off and filed for divorce. How many of you knew he was*

even married?" A few audience members clapped. *"I know, right. If he kept his marriage so quiet, what else will we be finding out about him in the next few days?"* She gave the camera a big grin like she'd just discovered weapons of mass destruction. *"We even have a picture of his wife with her new man, looking quite loving."* Two pictures flashed on the screen. The top one showed Melissa seated at a small table, holding hands with Rob. The second one showed the two of them hugging.

Darius inched closer to the television to stare at the photographs. The sound on the television faded into one long garbled sound that wrapped around his heart and squeezed the life out of him.

"She's very attractive, right? With the long lashes and those good pouty lips. And check out those expensive Ferragamo boots. I hope the new man can afford to keep her in the style she must be accustomed to. He must have big bank too." Sunny nodded. *"She didn't waste any time replacing Darius. The new man is good-looking, but he's no Darius. Well, since Darius is going to be single again, we'll have to keep an eye on him. This might get very interesting."* She wrung her hands like a witch casting a spell over a boiling cauldron. *"When we come back, we'll discuss some hot summer trends. Stay tuned."* She smiled unaware that the earth had stopped spinning.

Chapter Twenty-One

Darius sat still as a statue. Every muscle in his body coiled, bracing for a mile-high drop onto cement. Each brain cell pinged for attention. He stormed into the living area, tugging at the neck of his T-shirt to get more cool air to his burning skin. The confined space of the room wasn't large enough. He cut a wide path, including the bedroom, as he tried to digest what he'd just heard. This was not happening. Not to him. Not now. Not with Melissa. This was someone else's bad dream. His ears roared with panic.

The story had to be false. There was no way this could be his life. Maybe this was Dan's idea of garnering the attention of the press. But why would Melissa agree to these types of antics? What about the pictures? They looked real.

His cell phone rang. He darted back into the bedroom and picked it up. His mother's number appeared on the display. She watched Sunny Kincaid more religiously than him, so he ignored the call. He had no answers for her.

The pounding on the door roused him back to reality.

"Darius, are you in there? Let me in," Dan called.

Darius snatched open the door and glared at Dan. "What the hell have you done this time? You've gone too fucking far," he yelled.

Dan threw up his hands. "I certainly didn't put out this trash. Why the hell didn't you tell me you were getting divorced? Instead of letting a big mouth gossip break the news, I should have done it. I could have used a tidbit like that to our advantage."

Darius choked back the vile response swelling in this throat while clenching his fists. His fingers grew numb but he couldn't release them. "Advantage. Are you outta you mind? This shit has no advantages. This is my life. This is real." He fell on the sofa and turned his attention to the ceiling. His hands covered his face. "What the hell is going on?" he muttered.

"You mean to tell me you didn't know anything about this? I thought Melissa was on the up and up, a good one."

The muscles in his stomach ground to a hard knot. This announcement was as surprising to him as it was to the people seated in the audience. Was this how his father felt when he finally found out about his mother's betrayal?

He couldn't trust the words to come out coherent, so he only shook his head.

"What do you want me to do?" Dan balanced on the edge of the chair across from him and steadied his gaze on Darius. "Have you called Melissa to get to the bottom of this? Maybe the whole story was fabricated. You know how the tabloids operate."

"You're right. Let me call her. Stay here." Darius picked up his cell phone, carried it into the bedroom, and closed the door. Even before he dialed the number, his heart told him the story was true. The smiles, the tender words, all had been a farce. And like his father, the one person he trusted the most had betrayed him.

He pressed Melissa's contact button and held his breath. She answered the phone with the same enthusiasm as always.

"Melissa--"

"Darius, what's up? Is everything okay? You sound funny."

"I just watched the show." He tried to control the anger in his voice.

"Okay, I know. You always watch. But I need to get ready to get out of here. What's up?"

He cleared his throat. "You filed for divorce?" Anger burned a hole in his stomach. The line was quiet for several moments too long. Her silence was the admission he'd hoped against. He closed his eyes to digest the information. Red flashes of light popped behind his lids. He fell against the bed.

"Darius, it's not what you think." She was talking fast now as if by hurrying to explain she could soothe everything and stop their world from spinning off track. "I went to see a lawyer at the first of the year. I thought we were through, but I never signed the papers. I swear to you…"

He pulled his hand down his face, to stop the explosion in his head. "So, it's true, Melissa?" He wanted to sit up and rant, but his body refused to cooperate.

"Darius, it's not what you think. Let me explain."

"Don't you think you should have explained before you decided to see a lawyer? At the very least right after your visit. Isn't that what most people do? Before I made a complete fool of myself. I'm running around thinking we're in this great relationship and making plans for us and you're taking legal action against me. I guess it's just a coincidence she happened to have a picture of you and Rob hugging."

"What are you talking about? I don't understand."

"Melissa, don't lie to me, I saw the picture. I can't talk to you right now. This is just too fucking much."

"Darius, are you going to let me explain?'

"I think you've said enough. I don't know what you can say to fix this."

"But, Darius--"

He disconnected the call.

****

Melissa pulled the receiver away from her ear and stared at the phone. The finite tone in his voice had a ring she hadn't heard before. Her heart raced so fast it skipped several beats. "This can't be happening."

She dialed his cell phone number, but her trembling fingers pushed the wrong button and the text screen popped up instead. She cancelled the function and tried again. After one ring, his voice message came on. "Darius, please call me back. Let me explain." A steady stream of tears rolled down her face, the salty taste lingering in her mouth.

Instead of putting on her pumps and heading out the door like she'd planned to do only moments before, she sat on the edge of the chaise with the phone in her lap. There had to be a way to make this right, but she couldn't think of anything. Her thoughts refused to move past the anguish in his voice. The tears wouldn't stop.

Turbo sprawled out at her feet. An hour later, the two of them were in the same position. She'd dialed Darius's phone every ten minutes and left the same message.

"Please let me explain."

When his voice mailbox was full and wouldn't allow her to leave another message, she crawled into bed and pulled the sheet over her head.

Chapter Twenty-Two

Darius slouched in the chair while staring at the mini bar. Sweat still poured down his temples. Leaving everything on stage wasn't working too well. He wanted to walk away from the show so exhausted he'd sleep and forget. But after three weeks and seven shows, once the music stopped and the lights dimmed, all the fury remained embedded in his soul.

Without blinking, he took several short breaths. Deep breathing would have been better, but nursing the pain consuming him was more in line with how he felt.

One day, he'd wake up and feel normal again. He wanted to believe in the possibility. But as long as he held on to just a little of the bitterness, no one would ever be able to crush him, again. He ran his hand over his chest. Even though he couldn't feel the gaping wound in his heart, he knew it was there.

Without knocking, Dan charged in the room.

"Another great show. I know you're unhappy, but you're killing it on stage. And record sales are off the chart." Dan's enthusiasm was as uncontrollable as a puppy. His excitement only added to Darius's misery. He should be happy that his career was skyrocketing, but his personal life was dragging him into the undertow.

"There's no sparkling water in the fridge," Darius said without looking up.

"I just gave you great news and all you can say is you don't have any water?"

"I requested it in the contract. I don't want plain water. I asked for sparkling water. Can you get some up here?" Darius stormed out of the living room, into the bedroom, and slammed the door.

"You know, if you're going to be this miserable, you might as well go crawling back to her."

"She's got a name, Dan," he yelled.

"Yeah, but last week, you told me not to say her name around you. Make up your mind."

"Are you going to get the water or not?"

"I'm not your servant, but I'll see about it. In the meantime, you might as well change for the photo shoot with the radio winners. They'll be ready for you in about an hour. Then, we're going to the club and taking more pictures."

"Dan, you know how I hate doing those staged poses."

"We all have something about the business we don't like, but we do them anyway. Besides, you haven't been photographed since your divorce news broke. We need to let everyone know you aren't devastated by the breakup. So, smile pretty for the cameras." Dan's voice had an air or authority.

"Yeah, right." He flipped over on the bed and grabbed the pillow. "I'll be ready."

Tonight, he'd be just fine. No way would anybody know the pain lining his stomach. Unlike his father, he'd mask his emotions. Melissa would never know how badly she hurt him. Never.

After a few seconds, the outer door to the hotel room closed. Darius rolled onto his back. If life could return to normal just by not mentioning her name, he'd be fine. But it wasn't so simple. He reached for the phone and dialed her number. Before the connection was completed, he hung up and threw the cell across the room, where it bounced off a chair and landed on the floor.

A couple of beers and a shower had managed to chase away his moodiness by the time he jumped on the elevator and headed down to the hotel club. The thumping of the music could be heard in the lobby. Cameras snapped as he made his way to the far end of the massive property where the good times were well underway.

Dan motioned him over as soon as he stepped through the door. The crowd stopped for a moment, and then a roar of cheers went up. Everything he loved about the limelight was evident in the pulse of the atmosphere.

"They love you, man," Dan shouted above the noise.

"Let's get this party started." Darius waved his hands and everyone stood.

"I see you've decided to have a good time." Dan slapped him on the back.

He spread his lips and showed his teeth, hoping in the pictures his attempt would look like a smile. He posed with several fans and signed autographs. Melissa wasn't the only one good at taking pictures. He slipped his arm around the newest lingerie model and struck a stance for the paparazzi. Playing the man behind the mask was a role he thought he'd abandoned years ago, but as he positioned for the pictures, nothing felt authentic. But, he needed to try.

"So, I heard you're single now," she said without breaking her smile for the photos. "Here's the key to my room. I'm in 2122. I'll be looking for you." She kissed him and slipped her tongue into his mouth.

Before Melissa, he would have accepted the offer and rumpled the sheets all night long. But he wasn't that man anymore. He pulled away without making a scene. "Thanks for the offer, but I'm going to pass," he said as he moved to another group of fans.

Chapter Twenty-Three

Melissa sat beside the window of the chalet staring at the lush green acres of wine grapes. A butterfly hovered over the fruit ripening on the vine. As long as she stayed perfectly still, the pain wasn't so bad. Only when she tried to get back to normal did the piercing anguish rear up and remind her she'd wrecked her life.

Nobody deserved to feel this bad. There was a time when she could do no wrong in Darius's eyes. But she had a hard time remembering when.

"Aren't you going to come out of your room for breakfast?" Pam stood in the door with her hands on her hips.

"I'm not hungry. Eat without me," she responded as she returned her gaze outside. The tranquility of the Napa Valley usually rejuvenated her, but she hadn't left the house since they got here.

"When I planned this trip, I had no idea we'd have to spend it trying to pull you back from the brink of despair." Pam crossed the mahogany wood floor and sat on the bed across from her. Her tiny yellow shorts and flip flops were a perfect match. The white tank top accentuated her small waist. Seeing the gleam in her eyes now was proof there was life after a failed marriage.

Melissa reached for her hand. "I'm just numb right now. In a day or two, I'll be back to my old self."

Pam lifted an eyebrow. "It's been over a month. Look at you. You aren't eating, you aren't painting, you aren't doing anything. All you do is stare out of the window and cry like you expect to see Darius charging up the hill to rescue you."

Melissa shrugged a shoulder. His name was like a poker in her ear. Painful. "Did the university call again?"

"No, I told them you would be out for the balance of the semester. You can tell them what you're going to do for the fall once you decide. They were actually quite understanding."

Melissa nodded. "It's been a month. Pam, I haven't heard from him in a month." Tears filled her eyes. "How can he be so angry? The least he could do is return my calls, even if he never wants to see me again…say something."

Pam came to sit on the arm of the chair and rubbed her back. "You know I'm hardly one to offer much comfort, but you can get through this. No matter what happens, you can."

They sat together in silence for several minutes. The tears continued to roll off her cheeks and onto the thin gown she'd slept in. Every word Pam said was true. Sequestering herself away in the hills of the Napa Valley couldn't last forever.

Sooner or later, she needed to address her life. Darius had taken a position. She needed to adopt one too. The time had come to stop hoping something would be different. Stop hoping she could mend their marriage. Stop hoping for a miracle. Miracles only existed in fairy tales. It was time to stop hoping for one.

"You remember your sisters are arriving today, don't you?"

Melissa pulled her legs up to her chest and wrapped her arms around them. She nodded.

"You don't want them to see you like this, do you?" Pam tugged on her nightgown. "You're still in your pajamas at two in the afternoon. Let me bring you a cup of coffee while you go shower. How about that?" Pam stood up and gave her a hopeful smile.

Melissa unfolded her legs. "No coffee for me; it upsets my stomach. I'll meet you on the porch, but I'm drinking tea, decaf tea."

She made her way to the bathroom.

By the time she walked out on the porch, the sun had warmed the small area. She stepped beyond the shade of the veranda and allowed the sunlight to touch her skin. This was the first time she'd been outside since they'd arrived two days ago

"You look better," Pam said as she came through the door.

"It's amazing what a shower can do for you."

Pam placed a platter of golden brown pancakes in the center of the table. The smell whiffed to her nostrils, reminding her of childhood and happier times.

"Breakfast food for lunch. That a good idea. When did you learn to make pancakes?" Melissa slipped into the chair.

"What make? I called down to the carriage house and they made them for me. I did scramble the eggs and cook the bacon. Sorry about the crispiness. I struggled with the microwave," Pam said as she reached for the platter.

"What time will Asa and Dakota get here?"

"They called when you were in the shower. Their plane landed and they should be here in a few hours."

"I feel guilty dragging them all this way. I'm going to be fine." Melissa placed a tea bag into the hot water.

"Think of this as a girls' getaway instead of a rescue mission. We're all happy to be here for you," Pam said around a mouth full of food.

"Where's my cell phone?"

"I shut it off when we arrived. You weren't in any condition to take calls. It's near the television in the sitting room."

Melissa reached for the eggs and scrapped a large heap on her plate. Like a bird being pushed from the nest, it was time to spread her wings and soar. She couldn't continue to live in the shadows of her parents or behind the spotlight of Darius. The only way to find her happiness was to make it.

If throwing away their marriage was so easy for Darius, then she'd find a way to accept his decision. Mim always said behind every cloud was a silver lining, so now was the time to find her silver lining. She could remake her life any way she wanted and in any place she saw fit. And it wouldn't be on the west coast.

"You know what? I think I'm moving to Philly with you." She looked across the table at Pam.

"Get outta here. You are not. What about Darius?"

"Oh, yes, I am. Mim said everything happens for a reason, and maybe I saw a lawyer earlier this year because the universe was telling me to find myself and to stop being afraid." She ate a forkful of eggs. "I'm packing up my stuff and moving to Philly as soon as we get back to San Francisco. Darius can do what he damn well pleases with the house."

Chapter Twenty-Four

Melissa wrapped tissue paper around the vase and tucked the excess into the opening, making sure the fit was snug. She handed the vase to Pam, who placed it in the last of the boxes. "Okay, I think we're all finished, and it only took us a week. I couldn't have done it without you, Pam. Everything I need is packed and all ready to go."

Pam stood in the middle of the living room with her hands on her curvy hips. The room was nearly empty. "I figure I owe you since you let me stay here while all my stuff was on its way across the country. Besides, when I was falling to pieces, you helped pull me together."

"I'm not falling to pieces," Melissa huffed.

"Just because you keep your emotions inside doesn't mean you're handling everything. I know you pretty well, Melissa, and I bet you're still crying every night."

"Then you'd just lose your money, because I'm not."

"Okay, most nights then. You think I can't hear you down the hall."

"Bunking in the spare bedroom doesn't give you permission to eavesdrop on me."

"I can hear you without leaving the bed." Pam sat back down on the floor beside her. "I can't believe how this all turned out. I'm more surprised by what happened with you and Darius than I am with what happened with Steve and me. I just knew you guys would live happily ever after. If you two couldn't, then nobody can."

"I'm not co-signing on your statement. Look at Asa and Simeon. They are happy. And Dakota and Bishop seem quite blissful too. We just have to find the right person." She taped the flaps on the box. "I even understand why Darius is so angry. He thinks I betrayed him. And maybe I did. I knew I should have told him about seeing a lawyer. I kept waiting for the right time. I just didn't trust our love enough to tell him. Now, I feel betrayed. He should have let me explain what I was going through. But he still won't talk to me, and it's been months."

"Maybe one day you'll get the chance. You still love him, don't you?"

Melissa fought the tears collecting in her eyes and nodded.

The room minus the furniture looked just as abandoned as she felt. Not a day went by when she didn't still dial Darius's number. But she'd stopped sharing that information so her friends and sisters wouldn't think she was desperate. "I'll always love Darius. One day he just might forgive me. But, I'll never live in another person's shadow."

"And what are you going to do until then?"

"I'm going to start my life over again in Philly. I'm going to open the gallery like I planned, on South Street. I lost the deal with Vincent Michaels, another thing I can blame Darius for. Anyway, all this must be some kinda sign and I just haven't figured it out yet. I bet Mim would have a saying for this very thing, and I'm going to figure out what it is."

"You make starting over sound so easy."

"It won't be. With the gallery and moving, I have to live on a budget now. No more huge shopping sprees and designer shoes." She displayed her flip-flops. "I'll be fine and soon I'll start to believe it," she said.

"I still don't understand why we can't be roommates in Philly."

Melissa ran her finger along the tape, pressing it firmly in place. "The last thing we need is to become crutches for each other. Until we both are able to put our lives back together, we need to live in separate places. Our condos are only a few blocks apart."

"Still no word from Darius?" Pam asked.

She bit her bottom lip. "No. But he had Dan call to arrange pick up for some of his things. He was more interested in getting his precious record player than he was in hearing anything I had to say."

"Do you think you guys will ever talk? I just can't imagine ending a marriage without a discussion." Pam shook her head.

"It's been two months now. Talking seems so inadequate. The things we needed to say should have been said weeks ago." Melissa unfolded her legs and stood. She swayed and rested her hands on her knees until her head stopped spinning.

"Are you okay?"

"Yeah. I think I stood up too fast." Melissa took a deep breath.

"When are you going to see a doctor? The lightheadedness, the upset stomach, and the no appetite thing is getting old."

"As soon as I get settled. Can you blame me for being discombobulated? Look at my life." She threw her hands up.

"So, you get to keep the dog?"

"I think he would have asked for him back too, but you can't put him in a box and ship him. Besides, I dare him to take Turbo. I've spent more time with that dog than he has." She rubbed the dog's head.

Pam laid flat against the floor and placed her hands behind her head. "Aren't you just a little scared of the future?"

"I'm scared to death, Pam."

Chapter Twenty-Five

Darius stared at his cell phone. Sooner or later, he had to talk to Melissa, but the sting of her treachery wouldn't fade. Every time he thought he was ready, his heart would fall to the bottom of his stomach and remind him of memories he wanted to forget.

If all women weren't different, then how come both his mother and his wife were so much alike? Growing up knowing secrets had destroyed his parents' relationship, he'd done everything he could to avoid falling into the same trap. Now look at him.

"You might as well call her and get it over with. I see you checking your phone every few hours." Dan tapped his pen on the pad of paper on his desk.

"This is a new phone and a new number. Besides, it's none of your business, Dan."

"Everything you do is my business. It's been over four months, already. You might as well call her so you can get on with your life. You know you can't move forward until you clear up all the stuff in your past."

"Right after the last show, I'm taking a little break. I'm going to spend some extended time in Maui, maybe a few months. I have some songs I want to work on." Darius pushed his phone in his pants pocket.

"You didn't answer my question." Dan continued to tap his pen.

"You didn't ask me a question. You made a statement, and you know I don't take relationship advice from you. You've been divorced three times and you have two baby mommies."

"You are a lot easier to handle when you're happy."

"Stop handling me. What's up with the movie score?" Darius asked even though now he didn't care if the deal fell through.

"You got it, buddy. They loved the songs, and if you don't get an Academy Award for that shit, I'll give you back my salary for a year."

Darius chuckled. "You say the same thing every year."

"Yeah, but I usually say it about the Grammy. So, why don't you look happier? I thought this was the news you wanted to hear. You should be jumping up and down."

Darius dropped his head. "How can I get out of here without all the photographers seeing me?"

"You know you should be smiling for the paparazzi. Between the tour and the score, we're printing money like the Mint."

"Just tell me how to get out of here."

"The hotel has made arrangements for you to avoid the crowds. Just take the elevator down one level and use the employee entrance. You should be fine." Dan dropped the pen. "Hey, Darius, you're still committed to the tour, aren't you? Last night, you sounded fine, but you weren't in the stadium mentally. Can I count on you?"

"Hey, Dan, it's all about the music. See you at the Link tomorrow."

****

Spring in Philadelphia was always warmer than in San Francisco. Being back on Terra Firma felt freeing. The glue holding her life together was pulling double duty, but for now, this was the life she had.

She almost stumbled on a bump in the sidewalk and juggled the phone pressed to her ear. "What time are we meeting for dinner?" Melissa yelled into her phone as she hurried up Walnut Street.

"Asa can't get away until seven, so we're meeting at the restaurant. Can you make it to Bristol by then?" Dakota asked.

"Yeah, I'll be there. I'm meeting with the hotel banquet manager in a few minutes, and then I'll hop in the car and come down. If I get there early, I'll swing past your place and hang out until dinner." A line of news vans were doubled parked along the street, snarling traffic. She wove her way across the intersection.

"Great. See you then," Dakota said.

Melissa dropped her phone into her briefcase and pulled open the heavy glass door leading to the hotel lobby. The check-in lines were three people deep and several nondescript men and women loitered in the chairs.

She flagged down an unoccupied doorman. "Can you tell me where I can find the banquet manager? I'm late for my appointment."

"Ma'am, this place is a zoo today. He probably won't even notice."

"What's going on here?" She craned her neck to see around the crowd.

He hunched his shoulders. "I just work here. They don't tell me much. You can find the banquet manager on the Mezzanine Level. Take the elevator up one level." He pointed in the direction where everyone seemed to be heading. "I'll tell you what, to avoid the chaos, take the employee elevator. Follow me." He led the way through a narrow door just off the lobby and swiped the badge around his neck through the card reader. He pushed the up button. "If anyone asks you, just tell them Kurt let you in here."

Before she could thank him, he darted back down the hall the way they'd come and disappeared behind the door.

She adjusted her stance to stare at the illuminated numbers above the door, watching as the elevator neared the lobby. As soon as the doors parted, she jumped on and pushed the large M. If the hotel was always this busy, it was the perfect location for the gallery launch party. With three months until the grand opening, she had a lot of work to finish. At least the running around took her mind off the empty hole in her life, even if it was only for a few moments.

Since moving back to the east coast she hadn't called Darius. The urge to dial his number nagged her every moment of every day and sometimes she almost lost the fight. But, the little dignity she had left had to be used to rebuild her life. Her heart pumped his name through her veins, but her mind demanded she be strong and move on. Living in limbo may have worked for her mother, but it wasn't an option for her.

At least, this time, she'd found a reputable lawyer and started divorce proceedings. Now, all she had to do was arrange the launch for the gallery, see a doctor, and commission her first artist. The pain would eventually ease. Mim said trouble doesn't last always and she had to believe her grandmother was right. Being married to a man who wouldn't even speak to her was ridiculous. She shouldn't feel betrayed by him, but she did. Married people didn't walk away from their relationship without fighting to save it first.

She stepped off the elevator and hurried toward a bay of offices.

"Melissa, is that you? What are you doing here?"

Even though she hadn't heard his voice in four months, her heart double-pumped and every thought in her head disappeared. She looked up into the big, brown eyes with flecks of gold. Eyes she couldn't seem to forget, eyes that should have loved her always. The massive chest and broad shoulders of the only man she'd ever loved stood before her like a mirage.

"Darius, why are you here?" She stood still, afraid to move.

"My show is here in Philly tomorrow night. But how did you know I was staying at this hotel?"

She shook her head. "I didn't. I have a meeting...I'm here for a meeting." Her mind refused to cooperate. Her stomach was a jumble of anxiety. A ball of heat rolled up her back leaving her lightheaded. The conversations she'd planned for him vanished. All she wanted was to feel his arms around her. She swallowed and tried to regain her composure. Just when the idea of not seeing him again had settled in, here he was.

He stood ramrod straight and stared at her with his mouth slightly open and his hands deep in his pockets. His eyes pierced her as if he were staring at a stranger.

She took a step away from him. Overwhelmed by the warmth in the narrow hall, her legs felt weak. "Do you plan to be mad at me forever?"

He didn't answer right away. Instead, his eyes rolled over her, taking her in from head to foot. "I haven't given the future much thought. Forever is a long time."

She pushed her shoulders back, trying to be as nonchalant as him. "Mim used to say the same thing. But somehow knowing forever is equal to eternity doesn't help our situation much, does it?"

He widened his stance and dropped his head. "I just don't know how to wrap my mind around this…" He pulled his hands from his pockets and wrung them.

He stepped away from her.

She swallowed the bitter taste at the back of her throat. She'd rehearsed for this conversation hundreds of times, but the words wouldn't come now. The wound that was getting better opened up just as raw and ugly as before. She needed to get away from him. Far enough away where the pain couldn't reach her. Her vision blurred as her knees buckled.

"Melissa, are you okay? What's the matter? You look…orange."

"I can't…I can't." She slumped against him.
He lowered her to the floor and ran to the nearest door. "Call an ambulance. Hurry."

Chapter Twenty-Six

Darius hovered near the hospital bed. His stomach bounced like a truck on a road full of potholes. By now, the disappointment over her betrayal should have faded, but the eternal roller coaster was still riding him. If she wasn't dressed in hospital clothes and as pale as snow, he would have lashed out at her. Instead, he checked his emotions to deal with the current situation.

At first, not taking her calls was a way to punish her for keeping the secret. But the treatment had backfired on him, allowing his anger to grow. Seeing her now, he knew his behavior wasn't any better than hers, but he was justified in his reaction. The way she avoided his eyes said there was something blocking them now. Her ire rankled his rage and they were at an impasse.

He shifted his weight from one foot to the next. She was going to dig her claws in and make him pay. The constant tit-for-tat needed to end or what remained of their life would be shredded beyond repair.

Waiting for the doctor only added to the tension. Melissa kept dozing off, but he'd seen the alarm on her face. She opened her eyes to look at the door again.

"How are you feeling, Melissa?" He reached for her hand. Her smooth, warm palm felt limp.

"Darius, you don't have to stay. I know you must have something you need to do." She pulled her hand away.

"Okay. I deserved that. But, I'm not going anywhere until we find out what's going on." He sat in the nearest chair. "I thought you were going to see a doctor right after my last visit home."

She sneered at him. "Well, something more important came up, didn't it?"

He ignored the jab. "How long have you been sick?"

"I'm not sick. I haven't had much of an appetite since my husband left me, so I missed breakfast this morning. As soon as I get some food, I'll be fine."

"Oh, so, now, you're a doctor too. Nobody passes out because they missed breakfast, Melissa."

"Why don't we just wait and see what the doctor has to say?"

"Fine. Let's wait." He sat back in the chair.

She pushed up to a sitting position and placed her hands in her lap. "Darius, I hope we get to talk about our marriage one day. One day soon. But, until we work out whatever is going on with us, I really would like to handle this situation alone. And I want to be very clear with you from now on. I moved to Philly a few weeks ago and I've seen a lawyer to file for divorce. Before I was unsure and deep down inside I really wanted us to work out our problem, but you didn't seem to have the time or the inclination. This time you abandoned me, walked away. So, I'm sure it's the right thing for me."

Her words felt like cold water being poured on his head. The shell she was so good at erecting to protect herself was back in place.

"I figured you had something more important you wanted to get on with. Or, should I say, someone." His voice was as rigid as his shoulders.

She made a show of taking a deep breath. "Darius, I'm not angry or upset. I'm being a realist. We've got more reasons to be apart than we have to be together. Loving someone is not supposed to hurt this much. I'm freeing you and I'm freeing me. I'll have the papers delivered to Dan's office since I don't even know where you're living."

She punched the pillow and turned her back to him as the doctor walked in the room.

"Ms. Conroy, I'm Dr. Carlton. How are you feeling now?" The doctor was overweight and appeared competent. His hair made him resemble Santa Claus. Maybe he could bring them some cheer.

Hearing the doctor use her maiden name was like a whip across his face.

"Better. Can I go home now?"

He glanced down at the chart in his hand, flipping the pages and scanning them much too fast. He lowered the papers and turned to Darius with a questioning look.

"Hi, I'm her husband, Darius Bellamy."

"Soon to be ex-husband," she said.

Darius moved to the opposite side of the bed, across from the doctor. "What's wrong with her?"

"There's nothing wrong. She's pregnant. Soon, there will be an addition to your family." The doctor grinned.

Melissa's face was unreadable.

"A baby." He coughed. "Are you sure?" He spun around to face her while trying to manage his stomach in free fall. He grabbed the railing on the side of the bed. No wonder she didn't want him to stay around. She'd done it again, made him appear foolish.

"Yes, I'm sure."

Melissa ran her hands through her hair. "Pregnant? How can I be pregnant? I haven't missed a period."

"Well, it happens sometimes. But trust me, you're going to have a baby. However, you're severely dehydrated and we need to get some fluids back in your body. And you need to eat. Even when you don't think you're hungry, eat something,

several small meals are better than one large one."
He flipped through the papers again.

"Can I go home now?" Melissa jerked the
sheets off her legs, exposing her thighs.

"Not today. We need to keep you overnight,
monitor your fluid levels until they are back in the
normal range. Maybe tomorrow you can go home."

"I…I… this is too much." She rubbed her
hand against her forehead.

"Let's take it slow. First, you just get some
rest and let us take care of you tonight. Tomorrow,
there will be plenty of time to figure out all the
details. We need to find out how far along you are."
The doctor's reassurance seemed to help her relax.
She took a deep breath.

The doctor gave her a smile that extended to
Darius before spinning around and leaving the
room.

Darius observed her for several moments.
She resembled the vivacious woman he'd married
and wanted a life with, but all the secrets and deceit
were new characteristics. Ones he expected from
the groupies hanging on the fringe of the tour, not
from the woman he thought he cherished.

"Melissa, did you know?" He bit down on
his tongue. All he had to do was to get from this
moment to the next one without letting her see the
pain consuming him. There was a small chance he

could retain what little manhood he still held precious.

"A baby never crossed my mind." She released a nervous chuckle. "But, nothing's changed with us." The cold stare she gave him backed him up.

"I'm going to ask you a question, and I know you're going to get mad, but I need to know the answer." He cleared his throat. He tightened his hold on the bed and closed his eyes for a moment. "Is the baby mine, Melissa?" Asking the question was like stabbing himself in the heart, but he wanted to hear her say the words. If his world was going to fall apart, then let it happen before he started chasing dreams.

She turned her body in the bed to face him and he braced for her reply.

"Darius, you know me. Regardless of what we've been through, you know who I am. If your insecurities require you to hear the words, then yes. The baby is yours. Regardless of what images you've created in your imagination, rest assured this baby is yours."

He tried to hide the relief flooding his body, but the euphoric feeling was hard to control.

"Melissa, we both made mistakes. I had every right to be mad at you. How could you let me believe we were fat, dumb, and happy, and you were talking to a divorce attorney? And I hear about it on television. And the pictures, I saw the pictures, Melissa.”

“Your behavior wasn’t any better. You discarded me and nothing has changed because of an accidental run-in at a hotel.” She folded her arms over the white hospital gown and stared at the door. “What would have happened if I’d decided to have my gallery opening at another hotel and I’d never bumped into you? Were you ever going to try to reach me, Darius?”

Her words cut him. He’d been a coward. Instead of addressing their problems, he’d tried to ignore them. It was much easier to massage his hurt by pretending it didn’t exist. At some point, he knew he’d have to face her, but he imagined it would be to put an end to their marriage, so he’d stayed away. Delaying the inevitable. He’d tendered the idea their marriage was over and avoided facing the truth much like his father had done. All along, he thought he was different, so much more in control of his life. But the reality was he only controlled a small portion. She held the power.

“We’ll have time to talk about this. I don’t think this is the right place or the right time to talk about our future.” He needed to clear his head. His thoughts were playing a game of bumper cars, colliding into each other.

Her eyes filled with tears, but she didn’t speak.

"Please don't cry. I'll be here first thing in the morning and we can discuss what we're going to do. We are a long way from being done."

Chapter Twenty-Seven

Long after Darius had left her hospital room, she still had her hand on her stomach. Not once had she considered the possibility of pregnancy. What was she supposed to do now? Afraid to be happy, but too happy to be sad, she rubbed her abdomen and closed her eyes.

Just seeing Darius today was like scrutinizing old photographs and being nostalgic for the good old days. He had made her laugh. He had made her cry. He had brought her to life. But their relationship was like an addiction. The more she had, the more she wanted. Just when she thought she was breaking free of him, now, a child would tie them together for the rest of her life.

Old memories of her parents rushed in like floodwaters. She could hear her mother and father arguing about a baby. Her father's baby maybe. Spying on her parents had warped her. Melissa was willing to bet on that. All her adult life she had paid for hearing those grown-up details long before she knew anything about life. Her parents' arguments had colored every decision she made. For better or worse.

Dakota and Asa were much more forgiving than she'd ever been. But neither of them carried the burden of knowing all the details of their parents' life. How close they'd come to walking away from their marriage. If the accident hadn't killed them both, maybe they would have divorced.

She and Darius were like a mixture of fire and gasoline. Combustible. Each of them had dragged baggage into their marriage that had been heaped on them without them even knowing it. She didn't want to pass the same legacy on to their child. Their baby needed to have a chance of a normal life, with happy parents, not with two people just pretending.

"Are you okay?" Asa and Dakota said in unison as they rushed through her hospital door, disrupting her thoughts. They stood on opposite sides of her bed, but the same expression of concern was evident on their faces as they peered down at her like she was an invalid.

"Calm down you two. I'm fine. How did you find out I was here so fast?"

"Darius called me," Dakota said. "I called Asa, and here we are. What happened?"

"I'm going to have a baby." She gathered the sheet around her, finding safety behind the stiff cotton.

Asa's jaw dropped and she made a noise similar to a wounded animal. Dakota wrapped her arms around Melissa's shoulders and pulled her close while rocking her back and forth. In the cloak of safety with her sisters, she managed to smile for the first time about the baby.

"But what happened? Why are you in the hospital? When can you go home?" Asa reached out and touched her hand.

"Did you know? How many months?" Dakota clasped her hands like she was getting ready to pray.

She told them what the doctor had said and the worry in their eyes lessened.

"You know, I don't have any idea how many months I am. There's so much going on the doctor doesn't know yet. I guess I can almost figure it out." She held up her fingers and ticked off the months. "I could be as many as six months or as little as four."

Asa looked at her like she had a third eye in the middle of her forehead. "I'll call my OB/GYN and see if he'll take you as a patient."

Melissa pulled back the sheet and lifted her gown. "Check out my stomach, Asa. You've had two babies. What do you think? How far along am I?"

Dakota laughed. "I've never had a baby and even I know it doesn't work that way."

"Oh, shut up, Dakota. I know it's not scientific, but she might know when the stomach starts to protrude. See, mine is still flat."

Asa plopped in the chair near the bed. Her eyes clouded. She was always the serious one. "Melissa, you filed for divorce. What are you and

Darius going to do now? Raising a baby alone is hard. Honey, sometimes it's hard raising a baby with a full-time nanny and a husband."

Melissa's breath caught in her throat. She didn't want to think so far into the future. Whatever lay beyond the hospital bed for her and Darius was about as scary as a slasher movie. She squeezed her eyes shut, sending the vision away.

"Sorry I ruined our dinner plans. You guys will let me make it up to you, won't you?"

"Don't ignore me, Melissa. Now is the time to think about your marriage. Suppose you are four months pregnant. You don't have much time to get ready. And believe me, no matter how much you prepare, you won't be ready."

"Stop upsetting her, Asa." Dakota's voice was stern. Her eyes softened when she directed her attention on Melissa. "No matter what happens, we'll be there for you. We'll help you. Between Asa and Simeon and me and Bishop, we've got a tribe to raise this baby." Dakota beamed with happiness.

Melissa knew the smile she gave her sister was weak. She didn't feel as confident about the future as Dakota did. Two paths were laid out in front of her and neither one seemed like an easy trip. She could try to raise the child alone or she could try to save her marriage. The hollow feeling ballooned and she fell against the flat pillow.

"Guys, I don't know what to do. Forgiving Darius for just walking away seems impossible to me right now. And he hasn't asked for forgiveness. He's got so much stuff going on in his head, I don't know if I want to stick around until he figures it out. He doesn't trust me. He even asked me if the baby was his."

Dakota gasped and placed her hand over her mouth. "You're kidding, right?"

She shook her head. "If only."

"You know you've always been too hard on Darius. Give the man a break. We've all made mistakes. Even you," Dakota said.

Melissa lifted an eyebrow to her sister.

"Yeah, I said it. You are a long way from perfect. You should have been honest with him from the beginning. We all need to stop living in the past." Dakota finished and folded her arms over her chest.

"Visiting hours are now over. All visitors must leave the building." The announcement saved her from having to respond to her sister's edict.

Asa stood up and pushed her purse onto her shoulder. "We'll come back tomorrow to get you settled at home. Dakota's right. Whatever you decide, you can count on us."

Melissa watched her sisters leave the room. She released a long breath and rearranged the bedding to get comfortable. If she didn't take control of her life, someone would step in and do it for her, and she wasn't going to give control to someone else ever again. There wasn't much time to figure out a plan, but she would. She had to.

****

Darius stared at the dark television across the room. He hadn't turned it on, but he didn't need to. The images in his head were vivid enough. He'd fucked up a lot of things in his life but never something so important. Since returning from the hospital, he'd ignored the constant ringing of his phone and Dan pounding on the door. How could so much have gone wrong between him and Melissa?

Living from city to city and totally ignoring the only person who meant so much to him was unforgivable. He'd treated Melissa like a fan. As if she'd always be waiting for him in the wings, ready to deal with his new line of bullshit. But the look in her eyes last night said this was different. There was no forgiveness hiding behind her relentless stare this time.

To win her back, to win her love, would take more than a trip, a pair of shoes, or a few well-written musical lines. He dragged his hand down his face and sighed.

Usually, he was the man with all the answers. This time, he had none. But, the constant ache residing in his chest had vanished when he saw her yesterday.

He peeled off the clothes he'd worn the day before and showered. Afterwards, he dressed in a pair of slacks and a button-down shirt before calling the car to take him to the hospital.

As he caught the elevator to her room, he rehearsed his speech in his head. They had to at least try to figure out what went wrong and try to correct it.

When the doors parted, he took long, quick strides down the hall and through the maze to her room.

She wasn't in her bed. The rumpled sheets were the only indication she'd been there. Maybe something had happened or they were running tests. He spun around to return to the nurse's station and nearly knocked over a nurse carrying a tray.

"Excuse me, can you tell me where Melissa Conroy is this morning? She was in room 2204-B."

"Her doctor came by early this morning and she was released." The nurse hurried away.

Released? But where to? He had no idea where she lived. His heart thumped with his stupidity. He extracted his phone from the clip and dialed her cell. The number he had was no longer in service.

"Shit," he whispered before dialing her sister.

Without waiting for her to reply, he said, "Dakota, I'm here at the hospital and Melissa's been released. Can you tell me where she is?"

There was a long pause and he could hear muffled voices. "Darius, she doesn't want to see you right now. Give her a few days and she'll call you."

"Please, Dakota. I know I've screwed up. I just want to make it right with her. Please tell me where she is."

"I really can't. I have to be here for her right now." Dakota lowered her voice. "I promise, as soon as I can, I'll tell you where to find her." She disconnected the call before he could respond.

He looked down the hall to where three nurses gathered around the desk. As soon as two grabbed clipboards and walked away, he approached the remaining nurse.

"Excuse me. I hope you can help me. My wife checked out this morning and she thinks she lost an expensive bracelet while here in the hospital. I'd like to verify the address with you just in case it shows up so you can return it to us." He swallowed the panic in his voice.

"Name?"

"Melissa Conroy."

He waited while she punched a few keys on the keyboard. "I'm sorry, she left explicit instructions not to release any information to anyone about her." The nurse pushed one last key before standing up and leveling her gaze on him. "You're the singer, aren't you?"

"I'm her husband."

"Doesn't matter." She shook her head. "I'm not losing my job over your squabble. But, would you sign an autograph for my daughter. She loves you." She pushed a piece of paper across the desk to him.

"What's your daughter's name?"

"Juliette." She covered her badge.

He scribbled a greeting and his signature on the paper before passing it back to her. "Enjoy your day, Juliette."

Chapter Twenty-Eight

Melissa put her feet on the sofa and pulled the blanket over her legs. Turbo jumped up next to her and buried his head in her lap. Being back in her condo lifted her spirits even though most of the furniture hadn't arrived yet.

She didn't want to talk to anyone. Especially Darius. He had a way of drawing her into his web. Until she figured out her own path, she needed to stay away from him. Once, she would have dropped everything to follow his dream, but not again. The gamble was much too high. To do the same thing again could be her destruction.

"How long do you expect me to lie to that man?" Dakota dropped her phone on the table and glared at her. "He's been calling every day."

"Your alliance is to me, not Darius. So, I hope you'll keep my confidence for as long as I need you to." She rubbed the top of the dog's head.

Dakota lifted a brow. "He just wants to talk to you. You're carrying his child for God's sake."

Melissa sat up straighter and huffed. "I was in San Francisco for months waiting for him to call me so we could talk. I left him so many messages my fingers were dialing in my sleep. He doesn't like situations he can't control. He wants to march in and make all the decisions. But, I'm not the same person anymore."

"But this is different, Melissa," she begged.

"I know, Dakota. And I'm sure we'll have everything all figured out before the baby gets here. I promise."

"You know what the problem is? Both of you want to be the boss all the time. You need to learn the fine art of compromise."

"We have some problems, but I don't think they are caused by a lack of compromise." She shook her head and aimed the remote at the television.

"Do you want to talk? I'm here," Dakota offered.

"I don't feel like talking right now. I need quiet time to figure out some stuff."

"You've had a week."

Melissa was happy to have her sister around, but Dakota's marriage was perfect. What did she know about irreconcilable differences?

Dakota hopped up and started toward the kitchen. "I saw you roll your eyes at me. But, since you're in the family way, I'm going to let it slide. Let me fix you some lunch."

"Never mind, Dakota. Asa is bringing something later today when she comes back. I need more than hummus and crackers." Melissa frowned.

"Very funny, but you need to eat several small meals—."

The doorbell rang before Dakota could finish her sentence. Turbo bounded off the sofa and charged to the door. Another habit she'd have to break.

"I'm not expecting anyone. If it's not Pam, send whoever it is away. I just want to be alone." Melissa drew the blanket tighter.

The sound on the television was muted, but the picture was all she needed anyway. There was enough chatter in her head already. She watched Sunny Kincaid strut on stage, looking just as perky as the day before. Whose life would be on display today?

Dakota strolled back in the room with a dubious expression on her face. She was followed by Darius and Turbo. Instead of the hip-hop image he usually portrayed, he sported corporate executive attire. His shirt looked starched and stiff. The black onyx cufflinks matched his black slacks and shoes. Compared to her cutoff shorts and oversized T-shirt, they weren't dressed for the same occasion.

"How did you get my address?" she demanded as she struggled to sit up with her feet entangled in the blanket. She gave Dakota the once-over.

"Don't look at me. I didn't give it to him." Dakota hurried around the corner into the kitchen.

Darius parked his butt in the only chair in the room and crossed his ankle over his knee. The stormy expression on his face caused her shoulders to tense. He scratched the dog's chin without taking his eyes off her.

"Okay, you found me. Now what?" she huffed.

"Was your little stunt, payback?" He sounded like he could have been talking about the weather.

"How did you find out where I live?" she asked again.

"It wasn't hard. Several people know about the gallery, and Dan sometimes walks on the shady side of life. How long did you plan to hide from me?" His voice was even.

"I'm not hiding. I've been thinking." She folded the blanket and placed it beside her on the sofa. "I've never been divorced before and I've never been pregnant before, so I've got a lot of stuff to figure out."

"Since both involve me, shouldn't we try to figure it out together?" He remained in the same position, and the level edge in his voice indicated he was trying to stay calm.

She glanced around for Dakota to rescue her.

"You can't keep me away from the baby, Melissa."

"Keeping you away from the baby wasn't my intention."

"And what about the divorce?"

"Nothing's changed there. Just because we're having a baby doesn't mean we need to remain married."

"You sound pretty flippant. Don't you want what's best for our child?"

The heat started at her feet and climbed up her legs. He'd only been here a few minutes and already he wanted to control the situation.

She cleared her throat as the heat consumed her whole body. "Since I found out I was pregnant, I have done nothing but think about this baby. I'm not out talking to a group of artists right now because the doctor wants me to take it easy for a few more days. Please don't march in here and pretend you know or care about what's best for me. You haven't talked to me in over four months, so whatever you've got to say isn't important to me."

He leaned forward, and the menacing flecks in his eyes disappeared. "I'm not trying to upset you. I just want you to talk to me. I want to experience being an expectant father. I want to feel the baby kicking in your stomach. I don't want to just show up at the hospital after you deliver or on weekends designated to me by a judge who doesn't know me."

Darius wasn't the enemy or the bad guy. His request stroked her heart, erasing the bitterness surrounding it. "So, what do you suggest?"

"I'd planned to fly back to San Francisco and settle some stuff. But now…"

"Oh, since your tour is over, you were going to San Francisco because you just knew I'd be sitting there waiting on you." She held her breath to control the roar building in her stomach.

He looked away for several moments. His back teeth clenched. "I was coming home to sign the divorce papers you drew up."

She rocked from side to side. "I see."

All the divorces she'd seen were ugly matters fueled by resentment. She didn't want her and Darius to take those steps, but if he thought she would pick up her life and follow him back to San Francisco, then they just might become the next famous couple on the front pages of the tabloids.

"Spit it out, Darius. What's on your mind?"

He pushed off the chair and strolled to the balcony doors. Whatever was on his mind made her palms sweat.

"I don't want to be on the west coast and you, here on the east coast. It's just too far. You're going to think this is crazy, but promise to give it some thought."

"What?"

"How about I move in here until the baby is born? If I do, we'll have time to make some plans and I can help set up the nursery and participate in the doctor visits."

Her mouth flopped open. "Are you serious? We're getting divorced, why would you want to live here? You could find a place of your own. A much bigger place." She shook her head. "Not going to happen. I don't think that's a good idea."

He moved to the edge of the chair. A sparkle danced in his eyes. "It's a perfect solution, and it will only be for a few months. We can handle this split like two adults. I think we need to get all our old baggage behind us before the baby gets here. We don't want to scar our child the way we've been scarred by the battles of our parents."

She shook her head. "Nope. I can only see things going badly for me. Nope." She continued to shake her head.

He returned to the chair in front of her. With his elbows on his knees, he clasped his hands and leveled his gaze on her. "Melissa, think about it." His voice was soft, almost pleading.

"I've only got two bedrooms and two baths. Even though the rooms are large, we'd still be tripping over each other." She paused to make sure she used the right words. "The last thing I want to do is to have our child face life and choosing paths based on the things we did or didn't do. Just the thought makes me cringe." She searched his face, hoping he'd understand. He made his plan sound so easy, but stuff like this only worked on sitcoms.

"What have we got to lose, Melissa? If it doesn't work, I can always find another place. Besides, I don't think we ever agreed on who gets custody of my dog."

"Turbo is my dog now. You walked out on him, too." She patted the sofa and Turbo jumped up beside her.

"I might be able to win him over. So, what do you say about my proposal?"

Uncertainty buzzed in her head like thousands of killer bees. "I can't. We're too broken."

Chapter Twenty-Nine

Darius took the seat in front of Dan's desk without speaking. Nothing his agent said would change his mind.

"Moving in with your ex-wife is the silliest thing I've ever heard of. And I ought to know 'cause I've got three of them and wouldn't even consider an idea this crazy."

"You mean they wouldn't consider letting you. Besides, I didn't come to New York to get marital advice from you, Dan. I think the publicist has managed to provide a plausible story for both me and Melissa."

"Everyone is going to think you went begging to get her back. What will talk about groveling do for your image?"

"I don't care what people think. If this is what I have to do to be part of my child's life, then I'm doing it. Besides, I don't think Melissa and I will be spending much time about town. She has her gallery and I have to work on the score."

"It's your funeral man. Just don't say I didn't warn you." Dan picked up his pen and scribbled a note. He pushed it across the desk toward Darius. "Just give this number a call and they will deliver the stuff you requested. I'm meeting with a production company from Europe tomorrow. I'll let you know once we work out the terms."

"As long as they know I'm not available until after the baby is born."

"Yeah, I got it. Are you allowed to date while you're bonding with your new baby?"

Darius pushed out of the seat. "Man, you're too much. Remember the story is we're working on our marriage. If I start showing up all over town with a different bimbo on my arm, the press won't believe the release. Get with the program, Dan." He walked out of the office without bothering to close the door.

He glanced at his watch. He was going to be late for his father's big surprise. Once he was settled in the Town Car, he dialed his father.

"Dad," he said when his father picked up.

"Where are you, Darius?"

"I'll be at the restaurant in ten minutes. I'm stuck in mid-day traffic. Order me a dirty martini and I should be there by the time it arrives," Darius glanced at his watch again.

When the car pulled in front of the restaurant, Darius jumped out and ran inside. His father was seated at the table near the door with a striking woman cozied up next to him.

"Dad, I didn't know someone was joining us." Darius took the empty seat.

"I wanted to surprise you. Darius, I want you to meet Constance." His father wore the biggest smile he'd seen on him in years. Darius reached across the table to shake her hand. Her hair was as dark as her eyes and fell below her shoulders in a cascade of thick curls. She studied his father as if her breathing was connected to his movement. His mother had never owned a look with so much definition.

"Your father talks about you all the time. He even has me listening to hip-hop music now." Her voice was soft, barely audible in the loud restaurant.

"Well, Dad hasn't mentioned you to me." He gave his father a stern look. "But, it's nice to meet you. From the big smile Dad's wearing, he must be very fond of you."

"More than just fond, son. Constance and I are getting married."

Darius grabbed the water the server sat in front of him and took several gulps.

"I know this is a surprise, but we wanted to tell you together." Without taking his eyes off him, his father reached for her hand. Their fingers intertwined in an instant, like they'd been doing it for years.

"I guess I should congratulate you."

During dinner, the two of them talked about how they met and their plans for the future. Darius nodded and smiled in all the right places. If his father was happy, he could be happy for him. Thankfully, they'd decided to just go to a Justice of the Peace and avoid all the family drama.

"Dad, walk with me to the door. I need to get going." He gave Constance a superficial hug and headed to the door.

"You're sure about this, Dad?" he asked his father as he signaled for the car.

"My life has never been better." He patted Darius on the back. "I should have done this years ago. What was I waiting for?"

The deep furrow that always lived in the center of his father's forehead was less noticeable in the setting summer sun. Darius hardly recognized the man standing in front of him. He was so relaxed he could have been a car salesman.

"Dad, I was going to tell you later, but I guess now is as good a time as any. Melissa is pregnant."

"Son!" His father grabbed him and gave him a tight squeeze. "I'm going to be a grandfather. What great news! You have been the biggest joy of my life. I think some of my happiest times with your mother happened when she was pregnant with you." For a moment, he concentrated on the activity down the street like he was trying to recall the memory.

"I wouldn't know, but I hope to find out."

"Are you two getting back together?"

"I don't know. I'm trying."

"My advice, son, enjoy every moment. Don't miss a single event. Well, I better get back inside to Constance." He patted Darius's arm again.

"I hope we can mend our relationship. I've made some mistakes."

"Melissa is special. The two of you love each other. I can tell." He paused, and then nodded toward the restaurant. "Do you like her, son?"

"I do, Dad. If she can make you smile the way you are right now, then how could I not?"

Chapter Thirty

The doorbell jarred Melissa out of her trance. Trusting her instincts wasn't easy. Most of the time they led her down the wrong path. Allowing Darius to squat in the condo until the baby arrived was probably not a good idea. But his relentless five days of straight argument was convincing.

Sharing the biggest event in her life with the man she had no business loving seemed about right. Why should her life get simpler now?

She padded to the door, took a deep breath, and opened it. More than anything, she wanted to fall against him and hold on, but her dignity held her back. His expression was unreadable. She wanted to believe he'd stepped out just for a moment for a cup of coffee, instead of abandoning her for four months.

"One box? Is that all you have?" She opened the door wider for him to enter.

"With the stuff I had sent earlier this week and my things arriving later today, this is all I need." He sat the box in the corner of the living room.

"It's your record player, isn't it?" She came to stand next to him while he peeled back the flaps.

"Yep. I've read hearing music is good for unborn babies, so I thought I'd get our child used to

it now." He lifted the pristine recorder from the box
and placed it on the shelf below the television.

"You've been doing some reading, huh?"
There was a catch of resentment in her voice.

From his stooped position, he faced her.
"Don't look so surprised."

She crossed the room and sat in the chair. "I
am a little. I guess I never imagined you would get
into this part of having a baby. I always thought
you'd make a good father, but the nine-month wait
doesn't seem your style." She placed her legs over
the arm of the chair and swung her foot. She wasn't
angry with him but he no longer felt like her
husband either. Could they co-parent this baby in
harmony?

He connected the speakers and the power
along with a few other wires, then pulled a James
Brown album from the box.

"I thought you said soothing music. Don't
play oldies, she said.

He shook his head and pulled out an Earth,
Wind, and Fire album.

"Oh boy, from one old tune to the next," she
groaned.

"These are classics. My parents listened to
this music. I grew up on this stuff."

He placed the vinyl on the turntable and
dropped the needle in place. The sweet sound of the
kalimba filled the room, reminding her of the first

time they made love. Darius had insisted *Can't Hide Love* needed to be their theme song.

"That song takes you back, doesn't it?" He slid onto the couch.

If only she could visualize them just enjoying a Saturday evening like any other married couple. But the divorce papers were on the office table awaiting their signatures.

"So, now what, Darius?" She refused to be swallowed by a fantasy that didn't exist.

"Have you had dinner yet?"

"No, I mean with us. Since you're moving in, what's going to happen?" She placed her feet on the floor.

His eyes darkened as he came to his feet. The relaxed poise of his shoulder disappeared as he walked across the room and turned off the music. "You work on your gallery and I work on my score."

He disappeared down the hall into the small bedroom and closed the door.

Turbo looked at her with his head cocked to one side.

She gathered her hair on top of her head and leaned back in the chair. Mim had to be peering down at her from heaven shaking her head. This was one of the stupidest things she'd done in a long time. The apartment was too small for the two of them to exist together in it with all the emotions hissing and backfiring.

"If things are going to be ugly, I might as well get this over with too," she said to the dog as she made her way to the cubby hole just off the living room that she used for an office. The manila envelope had been delivered yesterday. She didn't need to open it to know that it contained her future.

She knocked on his bedroom door and waited for him to respond before going in.

He was seated with his back to the door at a writing table he'd purchased for the room.

"This arrived this morning."

Without turning around, he asked, "What is it?"

Her knees wobbled, but she stiffened her back and stepped inside. "Our divorce papers. You'll need to sign them."

"Leave them on the bed and I'll check them out later." His back remained to her but the edge to his voice said he was still angry.

"Is this how it's going to be between you and me? I can imagine the baby must feel this tension. Turbo won't even come in this room."

He turned to face her and placed his elbow on the top of the chair. "I'm trying here, Melissa. I never thought it was going to be a party, but I'm trying. I guess I didn't think I'd be asked to sign divorce papers on my first night."

"Did you think I'd changed my mind?"

His eyes stopped at her belly before returning his gaze to her face. Their eyes met for a moment.

"I don't know what I expected." He turned back to the desk. "I'll look at them."

"Well, I expect you to be nicer. So, if you can work on your attitude, I'd really appreciate it." She slammed the door and stormed to the master bedroom across the hall. Before she could close the door, he was there.

"Nice? You're asking me to sign divorce papers and I'm supposed to be nice? Maybe you'd like for me to order a cake and we can have a great big old celebration. How about that?"

"What's the matter? Is your ego wounded because I served you before you had a chance to serve me?"

He lifted his index finger and pointed at her. "Don't even go there with me. You started this show in motion. At least be woman enough to own it."

She placed her hands on her hip and moved closer to his outstretched finger.

"Believe me, I'm woman enough."

Chapter Thirty-One

Darius opened the cabinet under the stove, looking to find a frying pan. Without the convenience of room service, breakfast was his responsibility. He landed the pan on the burner with a thud.

Their discussion last night just proved living together while she was pregnant wouldn't be easy. Pregnant women already had to deal with mood swings, but by the time Melissa added her bias against him to the mix, living together could be like living in a war zone. He'd tone his attitude down a little. This arrangement was about the baby, not about their marriage.

All he needed to do was eat fast and get to the new studio before Melissa came back from her walk with the dog. After last night, it was obvious they hadn't planned this experiment well enough.

He was a jerk. His little outburst last night was not called for. Why he'd let Melissa taunt him was unexplainable. All those conversations in his head about how he was going to be cool and reserved were ditched the moment she challenged him for wanting to be there. Talking about divorce backed him in the corner.

He didn't hear her come in until the dog nudged his leg. "Hey, boy," he said.

Melissa's hair was pulled back into a messy ponytail, but she looked incredible. The thin sheen of perspiration on her face made her glow. The tiny, shorts exposed her firm legs, and all he could think about was the last time he'd laid between them. Five months was a long time.

"What cha' cooking?" She positioned her ass on the stool in front of him. Even though she didn't quite smile, at least the cold cast from last night was gone.

"Eggs. Want some?"

"Let me wash my hands. I'll be right back." He couldn't take his eyes off her butt as she dashed down the hall. Maybe she'd be open for a little sexual activity to fill some of the hours they needed to share.

When she walked back in the kitchen, the sweat was gone. He divided the eggs between two plates and sat beside her. "I know you'll think this is corny, but you have a glow."

"I was just in the mirror. All I saw was fat cheeks, a shiny face, and spreading hips. I hope I'm not one of those women who gain a ton of pounds, then have a baby only weighing five pounds." She shoved a forkful of eggs in her mouth.

"You don't have to worry about your weight. Turbo and I will make sure you stay healthy." He put his fork down. "What time are you going to the gallery this morning?"

"I'm there every morning at nine. Today, I'm meeting with two artists. If all goes well, I just might add them to the opening."

"Are you going to invite me to the opening?" he asked.

"I…I…I hadn't thought about it. I guess I never thought our lives would get intertwined just because we were doing this baby thing."

He put his fork down. "You're inviting people you don't know to your opening, so why not me?"

"What?"

"I didn't stutter. You know exactly what I'm saying. Besides, I've got swag that could add some cool to your stuffy opening," he teased.

"I didn't mean you couldn't come. Of course, you can come—I'd love for you to be there. Feel free to bring someone if you want." Her flippant comment hung in the air as she and the dog trotted down the hall.

"I just might," he yelled at her.

****

Melissa slammed the bedroom door. If he stepped foot in her gallery with a hussy on his arm, she'd pull every track out of the woman's head. She pulled off her clothes and placed her hands on her stomach while viewing her profile in the full-length mirror. The slight protrusion of her stomach was hardly noticeable. But the slip gown she had in mind for the party would not accommodate both her stomach and hips.

She picked up the phone and dialed her sister.

"Asa, I need your help," she said.

"Is everything okay?"

"I feel fine. My appetite is back with a vengeance. I think I'm putting on five pounds a day. I'm going to need something to wear to the opening that's big enough to go around my hips."

"Melissa, the opening is in two days," she squealed.

"I know, but this just happened." She paused. "Or I'm just noticing. I'm six months and I can't hide this potbelly anymore. Please tell me you can help me. And I want something super sexy."

"Oh, where is this coming from?"

"You know Darius is living here, and I want him to know what he's giving up." Melissa ran her hand over her stomach while glancing in the mirror.

"Melissa, must you always play with fire? You know you don't have to fight every battle. You can choose to let the minor ones ease on by."

"Asa, that's easy for you to say. You and Simeon haven't had a bad day in your marriage. I've had more than my share."

"Simeon and I have some bad days. But I'm not trying to cut him off at the knees. I love him and I know he loves me, so we find a way to work through the issues." She paused. "Stop by the boutique today, I think I have just the dress for you."

"I'll be there."

Chapter Thirty-Two

Melissa cracked open her office door at the back of the gallery to glance at the gathering crowd. Even though the gala didn't start for ten minutes, several people were already milling around in the spacious gallery, doing more talking than buying.

Before stepping out of her office, she turned to her sisters. "How do I look? Please tell me you can't tell I'm pregnant."

"You couldn't be any more radiant. The dress fits you perfectly. Asa's assistant nailed the tailoring," Dakota said.

Melissa ran her hand down the front of her gown. The seductive low-cut V-neckline with ruched bodice highlighted her ample cleavage. The empire waist and A-line skirt hid her hips. She twirled around and the full skirt billowed out around her.

"Asa?"

"You look fabulous, honey. Now, go on out there and celebrate your opening. Simeon and I have already found the perfect piece to go in the sitting room."

Melissa gave her sisters a wink before leaving.

Working the room was easy. Greeting guests kept her from watching the door to see if Darius would bring a date. She hadn't meant to taunt him, but his reply was just as surprising. Each time the door opened, she expected to see him come through with a tall, sleek model on his arm. She struggled to catch her breath as the idea settled on her shoulders. She didn't want to admit how much the thought hurt.

The night wore on. The room filled gradually with people. One glance around at the stark white walls revealed several empty spaces and several larger pieces with sold tags tucked in the corner awaiting delivery.

The few remaining artists gathered in the corner having a quiet conversation. She hurried to catch them before they departed too.

"Are you guys pleased with the way tonight turned out?"

"It was awesome. I sold out every piece." The only female artist in the bunch looked like she was about to burst.

"Then you need to get back to work and soon." She waved goodnight to them and locked the door as they exited.

Darius never showed. She rubbed her forehead. Maybe there was a bright side to his absence. They had separate lives. Living together didn't change the circumstances concerning their life. The divorce papers on the table were a testament, just in case she wanted to forget.

After a night of walking in four-inch heels, she was happy to have a car drop her off at the front door of her apartment. Of all the dreams she'd had, this wasn't how she had expected the big celebration to end, alone and exhausted.

She let herself in the apartment and dropped her purse before greeting the dog. From the entrance, she could hear music wafting from the living room.

Darius sat in the darkened room with a Corona gripped in his hand.

"I thought you might show up tonight." She tried hard to sound nonchalant.

"I had some business I needed to handle, and then I decided to just stay in and work on lyrics." He took a swallow. "How was it?"

She dropped her earrings on the counter without turning to face him. "It turned out great. We sold more than I thought we would. Which is a good sign."

"You sound surprised. You'll be a success. You always are."

****

Darius tried not to stare at her, but his gaze kept going back to her cleavage. The tiny straps of her dress barely contained the luscious bounty. He ran his tongue over his lips, certain she couldn't see him in the dark room.

Four beers within five hours gave him too much time to think and not enough logic to handle his thoughts. No matter how much he tried to ignore the images, Melissa was in every one of them. Now, she stood a few feet away from him in a dress that made her look like a goddess. His manhood pulsed with so much need he had to shift in the seat.

"Tell me about it." He hoped she wouldn't slip into her bedroom and close him out.

She crossed the room like a princess gliding in on royal shoulders. She sat in front of him, giving him a full view of her beauty.

Maybe the beers had him tipsy or maybe it was the sound of her voice, but the more she talked, the more his edginess slipped away. He envisioned every word as she recounted the details.

"See, it doesn't sound like you missed me one bit," he said when she finished.

"I would have liked to share the evening with you." She was getting ready to get up.

"Don't go yet. For the first time in months, we're acting like adults. I'm enjoying this."

"I wish you'd come tonight." He heard the disappointment in her voice.

"You never asked me. I guess I wanted to be invited, not an afterthought."

"Is that what you thought, that I didn't want you there?"

He hunched his shoulders. "I'm not sure what to think right now. Our life is in a constant state of upheaval."

"Maybe you've put your finger on what's wrong with our marriage. Instead of saying what we really felt, we were always sugarcoating things. Maybe we needed to vow to be honest with each other. No matter what happened."

"Are you sure? Honesty can cause some hurt feelings."

"I think we can handle a little truth. Maybe a little more honesty in the beginning would have saved our marriage." Regret gripped his heart.

They listened to John Legend sing about ordinary people, but nothing about him felt ordinary with her sitting so far away from him.

"My father is getting remarried." He blurted to keep her from leaving the room. "I saw him a few weeks ago and he seems really happy."

"Are you feeling okay with his decision? Or were you still hoping him and your mom would get back together?"

"No. I gave up on that idea months ago. The important thing is for the two of them to be happy. He's not planning a fancy wedding, which is a relief, so there won't be any odd moments."

"You know once the baby is born, you'll have to face your mother. She's going to want to see her first grandchild. You can't hide from her forever."

"I know and I'm not hiding. About the divorce papers—"

"Let's not talk about those papers tonight. We've got time." She paused. "Why did you get mad the other night when I brought them into your room? And remember, we promised to be honest."

He sucked his tongue and steeled his stomach. The only thing he had to lose was the most precious thing he'd ever had. "I don't want a divorce."

Her eyes widened before she hurried from the room. The sound of her door closing disrupted his heartbeat.

Chapter Thirty-Three

Melissa woke with the sun rise. All night, the only words playing in her ears like a broken record were, "*I don't want a divorce.*"

What was she supposed to do with his declaration? It was like selecting the winning lottery numbers after they were displayed on television. She had no magic wand to erase their past, or to turn this pumpkin into a fairy tale life.

She crawled out of bed and sat on the edge. With her stomach growling, she couldn't hide in her bedroom all day. She stepped out onto the private balcony. The view alone was worth the hefty price she'd paid, but she loved the big wicker chaise that allowed her to hide from the world for just a few moments. She stretched out and allowed the sun to kiss her skin long enough to warm her.

The bang on her bedroom door made her jump.

"Darius?"

"Come on out, I'm taking you to breakfast."

She wasn't certain breakfast was a good idea but twenty minutes later, she was dressed and ready to go. Darius wore a loose T-shirt over his jeans. There was just enough five-o-clock shadow on his face to give him a bad-boy quality. With his hat and sunglasses in place, his disguise was complete.

"I've already walked the dog, so let's head out." Darius opened the door for her. "Are you hungry?"

"I'm hungry all the time. If this keeps up for three more months, we'll have to take out a loan to feed me."

"I've got you covered."

They walked four blocks and turned onto South Street. "We're almost there. This little diner came highly recommended. I hear they have excellent pancakes and fried chicken."

"Can I get them both?"

Darius stopped in front of a plain storefront that didn't catch her attention. "You can have whatever you want. I want my baby's mommy to be happy."

The smell of fresh baked bread greeted them as they walked inside. A small bakery showcase displayed the biggest muffins she'd ever seen, along with lemon-frosted pound cake. She swallowed and tried to decide which one she was going to devour after breakfast.

When the server arrived at the table, Darius said, "Help us out, man. This woman is going to take a bite out of me if we don't get her fed right away."

After placing their order, she sipped water to fill the gnawing until something more substantial arrived. "Asa says what I'm feeling is normal. I thought I was trying to make up for those first few months when I hardly ate anything."

"From now on, I'll make sure we have something at home for you to munch on so you won't drool or snap at me. Are you going to pretend you didn't hear what I said last night?"

She sucked in a big gulp of air. "We promised to be honest with each other last night, and I wanted to think about my response before I answered."

"Maybe your most honest response would have been the one you gave me last night. Now, you've had an opportunity to script the good answer."

She wove her fingers together and placed them on the table. "There are things we want in life and there are things we shouldn't have. Discerning the difference is sometimes hard."

The server returned and placed two plates of pancakes on the table and two additional plates of bacon, eggs, and potatoes.

"This is enough food to feed a small army." Melissa picked up her fork and cut into the golden brown stack without syrup.

Half way through the meal Darius returned to his questions. "Melissa, we're not discussing candy or shoes. We're talking about our marriage. You can't lump everything together and pretend they are in the same category."

"How many chances do we give our relationship before we realize we can't get it to bend in a direction that works for both of us?" She reached for a strip of bacon and bit off a large piece.

"We keep trying. There's no giving up." He pushed his fork into his over-easy eggs, letting the yoke flow onto the plate.

From her peripheral vision, she saw a woman approaching their table. Other couples got the opportunity to enjoy a simple meal without interruption. Seldom did she and Darius enjoy the same luxury. If they wanted to discuss the state of their future, they should have eaten at home.

"Excuse me. Can I get a picture with you, Darius? I've got to be your biggest fan here in Philly." The woman, dressed in a green shirt and matching pants, stood at their table resembling a string bean. Melissa took another stab at her pancakes. Darius never ignored his fans, so she pushed a huge forkful of food into her mouth.

"Maybe, after we've finished our meal." His tone was casual, but Melissa could detect a bit of annoyance. He turned his attention back to Melissa before the fan had crossed the room.

"Did I just see what I thought I saw? I don't believe it. I don't think I've ever seen you refuse an autograph."

"I'm enjoying breakfast with my wife."

"My company has never stopped you before."

"People can change. Even me, Melissa. Now you know why I don't want to give up."

"I know, I just never thought I'd live to see such a miracle. If I could take this little moment and multiply it a thousand times, I could have been a happy wife. But I knew better."

"We've both made mistakes. You kept a secret that tore me apart."

She finished her breakfast, and for the first time in days, she felt satisfied. "I know my doctor will fuss if I put on too much weight, but I really must have a slice of frosted pound cake. I swear it's been taunting me since I walked in here."

Within an instant, the server placed the cake in front of her. Darius helped her finish off the slab, paid the bill, and escorted her out. He pulled his baseball cap down and put on his shades.

"You're really not going to sign an autograph for your fan?"

"I paid her check and autographed the back. The server will give it to her." He placed his hand on her back and maneuvered her through a crowded crosswalk. "Don't sound so surprised. I'm always nice."

"I've got a gap in our marriage that says otherwise."

Chapter Thirty-Four

Darius opened the car door and Melissa slid into the front seat. Since going out for breakfast last week, they hadn't spent much time together. Her snide comment had opened a wound he'd rather ignore. The small apartment made avoiding each other difficult, so they communicated in a series of groans, grunts, and gripes.

"When did you get the car?" she asked.

"It's a lease. Everything is so temporary I decided the car might as well be temporary too."

Melissa snapped the seatbelt over her ever-growing stomach. "I still don't know why we have to trek all the way to Bristol for breakfast. You know there are excellent eateries in Philadelphia?"

"Yeah, but your sisters, brothers-in-law, nieces, and nephews are all in Bristol. So, try to be on your best behavior and pretend this is the only thing you wanted to do today." Darius kept his eyes on the road. She'd been fussing ever since he told her how they were going to spend their Sunday morning.

"You shouldn't have agreed to it without talking to me first."

"Oh, boy. I didn't know we'd decided that I needed to run every little thing by you. You certainly didn't ask me before shoving the ugliest dressing table in the world in my room."

"It wasn't ugly."

"It was yellow, for God sake. Are you trying to scar our son?"

"We don't know if it's a boy. And we agreed not to ask the doctor, remember?" She placed her hands on her stomach. "Yellow and green are neutral colors. Haven't you come that in your reading?"

"I know you're having a boy and we won't be dressing him in *neutral* colors. The next time you go shopping, I'll go with you." He changed lanes.

"Yeah, right. You hate shopping, and you can't take your headphones off long enough to be bothered."

"So, today must be one of your bad hormone days, huh? You've been argumentative since you woke up this morning. Maybe you need a little loving to soften up the edges. Pregnant women can have sex, you know."

She folded her arms over her chest and huffed. "In your dreams."

"I know you want some of this. Stop pretending."

"Are you going to sign the papers, Darius? They've been lying on the kitchen table for a month. I know you see them."

"I do. I figure I've got until the baby gets here to examine them. Are you planning on going into labor early?"

"I would if it would make you get on with it." Even though she tried to sound upset, he detected softness in her delivery. Every night, she met him at the door with some new baby news or idea. Even if she wanted to pretend not to need him, she loved the attention he lavished on her.

"Aren't you happy with our current living situation? You're not ready to renege on our agreement, are you?"

"I can keep my word as long as you can keep your hands to yourself. I notice you're always staring at my breasts like you've never seen them before."

"I've never seen them so big. I swear they're calling my name."

"I don't have talking breasts."

"That's what you think," he mumbled loud enough for her to hear.

****

Melissa tried to remember if she'd ever heard anyone talk about how horny pregnant women could get. Her growing belly didn't seem to erase her desire for Darius. He strutted around the apartment bare-chested or in sleeveless t-shirts exposing enough muscle to still make her drool. If she had one more dream about climbing on top of him, she just might walk across the hall and take him.

"Let's get another thing out in the open while we're at it. You need to make sure you wrap a towel around your waist after you shower. I've seen your bare ass too many times."

His laughter filled the car. "Did you like what you saw?"

"How would you like for me to walk around the apartment showing my wares when you aren't allowed to touch me?"

"Baby, you can touch me anytime you want. No matter what I'm doing, I'll stop for you." He took his eyes off the road long enough for her to see the lust sparkling in them.

"You can't be serious for one moment, can you?"

"I'm deadly serious right now. Deadly."

He brought the car to a stop in Asa and Simeon's circular drive and shut off the ignition. "Remember, your sisters wanted to do something nice for you, so as hard as it might be for you, please leave your attitude in the car."

"How about you try growing a little person inside your stomach and let's see how pleasant you could be. I'm just praying I don't get nauseous while I'm here."

"You'll be fine. Sickness everyone expects. It's when you snap someone's head off that takes them by surprise."

Dakota opened the door before they even knocked. "I was beginning to wonder if you two were going to show up. Bishop and I got here an hour ago."

"Whew, trying to get your sister out of the apartment this morning was like herding cats. I should have let you all come get her." Darius allowed Melissa to walk into the house.

"Don't pay him any mind," Melissa said over her shoulder. "He's just horny."

"I heard you." Asa wiped her hand on a towel and gave Darius a hug. "She's just grouchy. Ignore her."

"I'm glad you all are having fun at my expense." Melissa placed her hands on her hips.

"Let's go out on the patio. Breakfast is all set up." Asa swept her hand toward the French doors.

Melissa led the way. The smell of food enticed her and even eased her disappointment for having to get up early.

"Surprise!"

Melissa stood in the doorway leading to the patio. A blast of heat rocketed through her body, leaving a film of perspiration on her back. She looked around at the crowd of people. Some of them she recognized, others were strangers. Darius slipped next to her and took her hand in his.

"You knew?"

"I did. But I was sworn to secrecy." He hugged her waist, pulling her closer to him.

"There goes our vow of honesty."

"I was honest. I told you I knew about it the moment you asked."

"Semantics, Darius," she whispered as Pam made her way towards her.

"We knew you'd fuss if we asked you about having a shower, so we decided to surprise you. From the expression on your face, it worked." Pam led her across the patio to the seat of honor.

"But why so early? Isn't a shower something you do in the last month of the pregnancy?" she asked.

"Yeah, but this way, you had no idea. If we had waited until eight or nine months, you'd be even more cantankerous." Pam smiled.

"Who told you I was grouchy?" She glanced up in time to see Darius disappear back into the house.

"Oh, we know way more than you think we do." The look on Pam's face left her with more questions.

Chapter Thirty-Five

The ride home was quiet, which meant she was exhausted or irritated.

"You had a good time, didn't you?" Darius maneuvered into the living room with a load of boxes nestled in his arms. Melissa closed and locked the door.

"Baby showers come with the territory." Melissa dropped her purse on the sofa.

"I'll get the other gifts out of the car in the morning." He placed the boxes on the table.

"If you leave those gifts there, I'll put everything away tomorrow. I'm going to bed."

"Want some company?"

She pointed a threatening finger at him. "Don't you dare." She marched down the hall and closed the bedroom door. At least she didn't slam it.

The gifts cluttered the table. He lifted the lid on the top box and removed the green blanket and matching towels. These were the things of a normal family. The family he wanted to be a part of.

He removed all the items from the boxes and folded them into neat piles. The tiny outfits, bibs, and socks were a jolt of reality. Until the shower, the baby was a fantasy, but the stuff on the table was like the pinch forcing reality on him.

"Come on, Turbo." He leashed the dog and headed outside. After disposing of the trash, he glanced down the street. For June, the air was crisp. With each step the anxious pressure sitting on his chest was less oppressive. And the way Turbo was prancing, he needed the release too.

He slipped back in the house an hour later. In spite of the low humidity, his shirt clung to his chest. After another look at all the baby stuff on the table, he turned out the lights and headed for the small bathroom designated as his.

The lukewarm shower didn't suppress his desire for Melissa. Afterwards, he made his way to the kitchen. A cold beer would help him rest. Melissa was asleep, so he didn't put on a towel as he made his way. He popped the cap on the Corona and took a sip.

"Darius!" The shrill way she said his name made his heart race.

He set the bottle down and raced to her room. In the months since he moved in, she never called him into her bedroom.

He threw open the door without knocking. The only light in the room flooded in from the hall. She was stretched on top of the bed with her gown gathered above her breasts looking ethereal. "Melissa, is something wrong?"

"The baby." Her hands were on top of her stomach.

"Should I call a doctor...I'll take you to the hospital."

"No. I'm fine. The baby is moving. He's moving. Put your hand right here." She pulled his hand on top of her swollen belly and topped it with hers.

"Melissa, don't scare me like that. I thought…I…"

"Shhh. Do you feel my stomach moving?" she whispered.

"No. I don't feel anything. Make him do it again." He climbed onto the bed next to her.

"I'm not doing anything. He's doing it on his own." She held his hand in place and applied more pressure.

"There, there it is. Tell me you felt the movement this time." She sounded like she was almost pleading with him.

"I did, Melissa. Does it hurt?"

"No. I thought it would, but it feels amazing. Absolutely amazing. I love it." Her eyes glowed with excitement.

For several moments they sat in silence. Waiting. The sound of their breathing was the only noise in the room.

"Promise me something, Melissa."

"Maybe. You might ask for the impossible. I can't make blind promises. There is too much at stake."

"Don't hold my actions against me and I won't hold your actions against you. I mean it, Melissa."

She nodded agreement. "Sounds easy enough. In fact, I think forgetting the past is a good idea. Because I want our child to grow up knowing no matter what's going on between us, he will be loved."

"I don't think he will have to worry about how we feel. I love him already and he's not even here yet." He looked into her eyes when he spoke.

"I think that's the way parenting works." She released a sob.

"Why are you crying; this is a good thing, isn't it?" Darius pulled her into his arms.

"Yeah, but there's so much. I wasn't planning to get pregnant and I think I'm just overwhelmed." She sobbed louder. "What do I know about babies?"

"I'm here for you. We are going to do this together. Tell me what you need."

"Hold me, please."

She smelled liked soap and sunshine. He didn't move, even after the kicks stopped. Melissa was breathing so soft it was several minutes before he realized she'd fallen asleep.

Chapter Thirty-Six

Melissa opened her eyes. She was lying on her side and Darius had his arm wrapped around her waist. Her nightgown rested above her stomach. She tried to slip out of bed without waking him. A few more minutes in this position and trouble would be next.

"Where are you going?"

"I'm pregnant. I gotta pee."

He moved his arm. "Are you feeling better this morning?"

"Not as good as you evidently." She pointed to his erection.

"Why don't you hurry back and help a brother out." He put his hands behind his head and bared his chest. Last night, nestling in Darius's arms reminded her of one of the things she missed.

Instead of going back into the bedroom, she turned on the shower and stepped under the water. Most of the night she'd pretended to sleep. But every time his rod stiffened against her, she'd wanted to reach for him. He probably didn't even know what his body was doing, but she caught every note. If only she could get her body to obey her mind. Not only had the baby taken over her appetite, her sexual desire had taken over her ability to think rationally.

She adjusted the temperature to as cool as she could stand it and stepped inside the stall. For several minutes, she allowed the water to wash over her body and relieve her hot skin. Water cascaded over her shoulders, and her heart, flooding her body until the overwhelming desire for Darius began to decrease.

When she stepped out, she was in control. She wrapped herself in a towel and peaked into the bedroom. The bed was empty. At least she would be able to dress without him staring at her or having to order him out of the room.

She pulled on shorts and a tee shirt, then strolled into the kitchen while trying to control her damp hair with a scrunchie. Not her best fashion statement, but eating was more important than her appearance.

"You folded all those clothes? And look how neat the stacks are."

"Yeah, I figured we needed to get some kind of order around here. I hope you didn't want to keep any of the boxes. I took them all out last night." He pushed the lever on the toaster.

"Thanks, Darius. That was sweet of you. And now you're cooking?"

"I notice if you eat on time, you are a lot happier. I'm doing my part for world peace." He placed a plate in front of her.

She sat at the glass table and popped a strip of bacon into her mouth. "I can't argue with your logic. The eggs are cooked just right."

He also poured a glass of milk and set it in front of her before sitting down. "Do you want to talk about last night?"

"What part? My fears or the way you poked me all night long?"

"The poking couldn't be helped. You slept with your butt against me. But I was talking about what you said. About being worried."

She smeared the toast with a large glob of strawberry jam and took a bite. After swallowing, she said, "I worry about being a good mother. The gallery is new/. It needs my attention. But, the baby comes first, so I don't know how I'm going to swing everything."

"And what do you think I'll be doing while you're doing all your stuff?"

She put her fork down. "I can't make assumptions about us. We are in a state of limbo. You keep ignoring the divorce papers, but everything between us is the same."

His eyes darkened. "Melissa, sometimes I don't think you're even trying."

"Trying what? We've been living in this two-bedroom condo for over a month and we're both still alive. You're not giving me the credit I'm due."

"I think you're failing to give me my props. My hours at the make-shift studio across town are regular. I'm home every night, whether you show up for dinner or not." He pushed out his chest. "I'm even cooking for you. And all this from a man who used to get his meals from a can."

She dropped her eyes to her empty plate. He was right. His transition back into her life had been so seamless she hadn't had a chance to resist. On slow nights at the gallery, she left closing to her assistant, to come home and watch baseball with him. When had her life changed course?

"You're right. I guess I saw it but didn't fully understand everything you're doing. But, I'm not ready to take your hand and run off into the sunset. You have to understand my reluctance. I still want to take one day at a time. Just having a baby is enough to handle right now."

He pushed back from the table, nearly tipping his chair over. "I cooked. You get to load the dishwasher."

Turbo followed him out of the kitchen, and minutes later, the front door closed behind them.

In the silence of the apartment, she cleaned the kitchen. Mim always said a tiger doesn't change his stripes. But, Darius resembled someone different. Instead of putting himself first, he actually thought about her comfort first. Even last night, he had held her until she fell asleep.

She picked up the baby clothes and walked back to her room. After placing them on the dresser, she gathered her drawing supplies and stepped onto the balcony. Without any visible neighbors, she settled into the chaise and sketched a new version of the man she married.

****

Darius opened the apartment door and Turbo bounded inside. The place was quiet. Melissa had to be hiding in her room. He placed the leash in the entry closet.

Since she was avoiding him, he could listen to any oldies he wanted. He selected a Diana Washington and Brook Benton single and placed it on the turntable. While the two crooned *You Got What It Takes,* he flopped in the chair and laced his fingers across his stomach.

His understanding of pregnant women was minimal, but Melissa had created a new class. There were at least two more months before the baby arrived, and if she thought he would spend them kissing her feet, she was mistaken.

He pushed off the chair and stalked down the hall. He knocked on her bedroom door but entered before she could respond. The room was empty, but the door leading to the balcony was open.

"We need to talk."

She put the tablet down and lifted her sunglasses. "Okay, what about?"

He sat beside her. "You're not running the whole show. I know you think you have indignation on your side, but so do I."

"Go on. You're wearing your serious face, so you might as well get what's bothering you off your chest." She smirked.

"What's so funny?"

"You are. You could bust a seam right now, couldn't you?"

"I'm really trying, Melissa. We haven't had a major blow up since I moved in. But, you only want to focus on the past. What do you expect from me, from us? You can't fall into happiness. It's something you build with the trials and tribulations of life."

She adjusted her position on the chair to face him. "How many trials do you have to experience before you walk away?"

"I don't know. I'll have to ask my mother." He had to squint against the sun to see her.

She ran her finger across his chin. "You need to shave."

Melissa could find a way to maneuver out of a grave. Her smile and touch made the point of his conversation less important.

"I don't know what's going on. I had everything all planned out, and you showed up again." She trailed her hand through his stubble.

"No, you showed up. And I'm glad you did."

She lifted an eyebrow but didn't respond.

The slow crawl of her hand under his shirt kindled a slow simmer in the center of his soul that radiated to every extremity.

"Do you know what you're doing?" He couldn't hide the desire in his voice.

"I know I'm horny as hell and you're here." She pressed her lips against his neck and climbed into his lap.

"Aren't you worried about your neighbors seeing you?"

"Nobody can see us." She continued to kiss his neck, darting her tongue along her flesh.

"In that case…" He lifted her shirt. She extended her arms and slipped out of the top. Without a bra on, her large, heavy breasts filled his palms. He hoisted her higher with his knees. With gentle pressure, he rubbed his thumb over one nipple while circling the other with his tongue.

"Take off your shirt." She pushed her hand into the elastic of his pants and held his rod with a firm hand.

He lifted her up.

"What are you doing?" She swung her legs off the chaise and stood.

"I was going to carry you inside." He removed his clothes.

"Uh uh. I want to make love right here." She pulled off her shorts. With the sun behind her, every curve was accentuated.

He ran his hands along her silhouette. "You are gorgeous."

"I'm fat. Why are you staring at me like that?

"Because you've never looked more beautiful. You're carrying my child and you I know now that I adore you. And I'm not afraid of that feeling anymore." The emotion swelling in his chest was powerful. The feeling of being vulnerable was both extraordinary and scary.

"In all the right places." He cupped his hands behind her head and lowered his mouth to her. She parted her lips just enough to accept his tongue as he laid her down on the chaise.

All he wanted to do was please and love her. He ran his tongue along her collarbone, then between her breasts. She arched her back as he continued his descent to the sweet spot between her thighs. Each time she called his name, it sounded like a song.

With each slow steady stroke, she released a groan that stroked his desire too. She grabbed his earlobes. Her legs tightened around him and her body jerked with tiny spasms.

When her body relaxed, she eased her hips down on the chair and loosened her hold on him. "Oh, Darius."

He kissed each side of her inner thighs. "Yes."

"What are we doing? This isn't going to help us," she said.

"Well, it certainly didn't hurt us."

She flipped on her side to face him. "You know what I mean. Sex confuses everything."

The morning sun moved behind a cloud, allowing the terrace to cool just a bit. There weren't any easy answers on what would happen next, and he was okay with not knowing. The casual pattern they'd slipped into worked. For now, he didn't need to pull back the curtain and examine life closer.

Chapter Thirty-Seven

Sitting in her small office tucked into the back corner of the gallery, Melissa wrote baby names across the lined paper. All of them male. Darius was so certain she was carrying a boy she believed him.

Darius Manning Bellamy, Jr. was written larger than the others. But with so much uncertainty circling overhead, she positioned a big question mark next to the moniker.

The blissfulness of the last few weeks was enough to make her wish the dream could continue. But, wishful thinking was foolish. Their relationship was like a bumpy road. When they were connecting, nothing in life was better, but when they steered off course, the pain was almost too much to bear.

Darius was warped like a vinyl record left sitting in the sun too long. All the things she'd found quirky and loveable about him in college had amplified when other real life issues piled on. But as much as she tried, she couldn't stop loving him.

Every night since they'd returned from the baby shower, he slept in the king-sized bed with his hand draped over her stomach. Their pregnancy love-making had intensity to it, almost as if they were trying to get enough of each other to last through a drought. And maybe that's exactly what she was trying to do. Sooner or later, they'd have to make some decisions and she had no idea which path they'd choose.

She dropped the pen. Enough daydreaming, she had a lunch date with Pam in ten minutes in the park.

She called out to her assistant as she left the gallery. The garden was only a few blocks away, so she walked. The temperature was pleasant. The clear day just might help her clear her head. She should be focused on motherhood, not all the eating and sex whirling around her for attention.

Pam wasn't there when she arrived. After she found an empty spot on a bench, she pulled her cellphone from her purse and dialed Darius.

His phone rang several times before his recording came on. She ended the call without leaving a message just as Pam arrived.

Pam bounded into the park with their deli order gripped in her right hand and her purse slung over her shoulder. Watching her friend come back to life was one of the joys of being in Philly. The other was being close to her sisters again. At least Darius hadn't mentioned moving back to the west coast. For the first time in her adult life, she felt like she was running her life instead of flopping around in someone else's.

"Ms. Pamela, thank you for suggesting we eat outside. I haven't done this in so long. You look absolutely radiant," she said to her friend. "Does your new attitude mean you've forgotten all about Steve?"

Pam dropped her purse on the bench between them and extracted sandwiches and chips from the greasy bag. "Actually, I have. I haven't had the urge to call him in months. Whew! I didn't think I was ever going to get beyond my feelings for him."

"Dating anyone?" Melissa asked.

"I'm dating everyone. If they have the sense enough to ask me out, then I always say yes. I had a few bad dates, but I'm having fun. Don't make me ask what's going on with you and Darius. How are the living arrangements? You two resembled a happy couple at the shower."

Melissa unfolded the napkin and placed it in her lap. "We've started sleeping together," she said without making eye contact.

"Like with your eyes closed, or are we talking about something more?" Pam moved closer and lowered her voice. "Spill the story."

"More."

Pam slapped her palm against her forehead. "I knew it. The way he was all over you, making sure you had everything you needed. And I swear he stared at you the whole time you were there like you were something good to eat. After all the lectures you gave me. Don't you follow your own advice?"

"Oh, shut up. We hadn't slept together before the shower. We started after. So, now that I've blown holes in your theory, can I say something?"

"Sure. I'm sure you have a good reason for sleeping with a man you plan to divorce."

"I didn't mean for this to happen. And I'm keeping my emotions guarded."

"That's bull and you know it." Pam gave her a piercing stare.

"I'm pregnant. I'm horny. I wanted him. I can't help it, Pam. What am I supposed to do? He's living in the house with me. I was seeing him naked practically every day. He's so sweet and takes care of me. He's being perfect." Melissa tore the cellophane from the tuna sandwich and took a bite.

"Do you know what you're doing?" Pam popped the top on the sodas, then ripped open the chips.

"No. I have no idea. Right now, I'm letting my libido lead the way. I figure I have plenty of time to be responsible when the baby gets here."

Pam shook her head. "If only life worked the way we wanted it to." She removed one slice of bread from her sandwich before biting into the turkey. "Maybe he's changed."

"But will the change stick this time or will he backslide to his selfish self when he starts touring again after the baby is born?"

"That's a chance you'll have to take. At least with Darius you know what you've got. This dating thing is tough. From one date to the next, I see all kinds of kooks. The crazy you know is better than the crazy you don't know." Pam passed the chips to her.

"I think for now I'll just enjoy whatever this is we have. At least while I'm pregnant I can't get pregnant again."

****

The apartment was quiet when Melissa opened the door. Turbo didn't even come charging around the corner to greet her. She placed her things in the closet and slipped out of her shoes. The cool feel of the hardwoods against the soles of her feet was a welcome relief. Maybe it was time to switch to flat shoes.

"Anybody home?" she called out as she entered the kitchen.

"Coming." Darius' voice came from the small bedroom that was supposed to be his, but he'd abandon it when he started sleeping next to her.

She filled a glass with tap water and drank it all without stopping.

"Come here, I have something to show you." Darius reached for her hand.

"What's for dinner? I'm hungry."

He lifted a brow and gripped her hand tighter. "Woman, do you think about anything other than food?"

"No. Am I supposed to?"

"We'll go out after I show you this. Close your eyes."

"I'm not walking around with my eyes closed. With this belly, I'm having a hard enough time keeping my balance." She pulled her hand away.

"Trust me."

She allowed him to lead her down the hall. She held out the hand he wasn't holding just in case. When they slowed, she said, "Can I open my eyes now?"

He released her hand for a moment. "Okay, now."

Inside the bedroom, in the center of the floor, was the crib she'd admired a few weeks ago.

"Oh, Darius, it's beautiful." She walked around the crib, running her finger along the side. The last several months had been perfect, like she'd finally landed in the right fairy tale. She made her way back to Darius and wrapped her arms around his neck. "Thank you. I don't know what else to say."

"You've said plenty." He kissed her on the mouth. The tenderness in his touch melted away the last vestiges of anger she had for his abandonment.

She pulled away just enough to see his eyes. "Did you put the crib together?"

"Are you kidding? I had them assemble the crib when they brought it in, and then paid them to take the full-size bed away to storage." He wrapped his arm around her waist and turned her to face the wall. The matching dresser and changing table were nestled against the wall. Tears stung her eyes. She was going to start crying.

"I don't know what to say. I'm surprised." She wiped at the tears as they landed on her cheeks. "You're being so nice. I don't know…"

"I promised to be here for you." He put both arms around her and planted his mouth over hers. His tongue was gentle just like his arms were around her waist.

"Now, go change your clothes; we're going out tonight. Wear something comfortable."

"Where are we going, out to eat?"

"Of course I'm going to feed you, but we're going to have some fun too." He tapped her on the butt. "Hurry, we don't want to be late."

Chapter Thirty-Eight

Darius escorted Melissa to the waiting limousine. For the past two months, he'd wanted all the attention focused on Melissa. She deserved to be treated like a princess on a pedestal. The last two years of his career had driven him to become someone he hardly recognized; no wonder she was ready to walk away from their marriage.

"Darius, you said dress casual. Now, I think I'm under-dressed," she said.

The driver held the car door open and they slid into the back seat.

"You look perfect. I've never seen another woman wear maternity clothes so well." He put his hand on her stomach.

"You like feeling him kick, don't you?" She put her hand on top of his.

"When I feel him moving, he's Darius Jr., not just a baby. Plus, you can't fuss when I'm just trying to feel my child versus trying to feel you up."

She gave him a playful swat. "So, where are we going, and what is the surprise?"

"Let me see. Should I tell you now or make you wait?" He pretended to think about it. "I think you should wait." He put his hand back on her stomach. "How is the gallery?"

"I sold my second piece today, the abstract of the Brandywine River. Even though the guy could have obviously paid more, I let him haggle me down. I'll need to bring in some more artists soon or the walls will be bare. I didn't take into consideration the lead time to get quality work. But, I know you don't want to hear about the gallery."

"I really do, Melissa." He rolled his hand over her belly. "Thank you for putting up with me. I know I'm damaged, but I'm trying to be better."

She bit down on her lip and nodded.

"We've both got some stuff to deal with. But, you have way more than me." She laughed and cut the tension.

The car slowed in front of the small, family-owned steak-house restaurant they'd found one night when she had to eat something and it had to be good. His stomach roared like a turbulent ocean. After two months of shining the spotlight on her, tonight, he wanted to showcase their love. The public needed to see them as a couple. Even though divorce was still a possibility, his world would always revolve around her, and if the world knew about them, then maybe, one day, she would too.

"Darius, I'm not dressed for this place. Look at me, in maternity Capri pants and a knit top. I should have worn a dress and heels. I'm wearing flats that barely match my outfit." She stuck out her foot in protest as he held the car door open for her.

"You look perfect. I'm wearing jeans, so we're fine."

The driver hurried to the restaurant entrance and pulled the door open for them. As soon as they entered, he could hear the buzz of people inside. Once they walked past the bar into the large dining room, the clapping began.

"What is going on? What are we celebrating?" Melissa stopped, the puzzled expression on her face demanding an explanation.

Before he could explain, Dan materialized from the group gathering closer. "Did he tell you the good news?"

"Not yet, I wanted to tell her with everyone present." He put his hand around her fast disappearing waist. Never had she felt so good in his arms.

"Do you see your sisters?" He pointed them out in the crowd, along with Pam. "And see, everyone dressed casual. Even Asa is wearing jeans."

Dan clapped his hands and everyone quieted. "I wanted to throw a little party for Darius. His second album - *Liquid Gold* - just went multi-platinum. He has sold over two million copies." The crowd roared with applause. Dan hushed them by waving his hands. "Wait, there's more. Tomorrow, we'll sign the biggest endorsement deal ever recorded for the record industry. I won't mention who the lucky endorser is since we don't ink the deal until tomorrow. Let's just say they're so happy to have him on board they're sponsoring this get-together tonight and they want us to have a good time. So with that, bring it on."

The music grew louder just as a stream of servers with loaded platters pushed through the double doors leading from the kitchen. The choreographed scene came straight out of Dan's play book. The two of them were crushed by a wall of people. He refused to let her slip away.

"Please stay by my side tonight. The only reason I allowed Dan to throw this party is because I thought you might come with me."

She cupped his face and kissed him on the mouth. Instead of the peck she intended, he deepened the kiss, savoring her essence. Her stomach kept him from holding her as tight as he wanted.

After a few moments, she pulled away. "Congratulations, baby. You've worked so hard and you deserve this. I see your dad and mom are both here too. That's great. This is your moment. Go mingle with everyone; I'll be fine."

"Nope. I'm not leaving your side." He held her hands as the crowd gathered around them.

"Darius let me get you a drink; what are you having?" Dan yelled as Darius's mother approached.

"I'm drinking the same thing Melissa's drinking, soda."

"Son, I'm so proud of you." His mother kissed his cheek. "Melissa's pregnancy agrees with you. And obviously, it agrees with the two of you. I never believed that nasty old business about you getting divorced. You two are so in love I can feel it." She placed her hand over her heart.

****

Melissa absorbed his mother's words without responding. She'd made the statement with such certainty she left no room for doubt. Melissa caught a quick glimpse of Darius, his face was expressionless. Were the two of them pretending for the sake of the baby?

"I hate to pull him away from you, Melissa, but I need him for just a moment," Dan said. "I'll make sure I bring him right back."

"Do you mind, honey?" Darius released her hand for the first time since they arrived. He looked reluctant to leave her side.

"Go, please. I was beginning to wonder how I was going to get into the ladies room with you." She laughed.

As soon as he disappeared in the crowd, she found her sisters. "Meet me in the bathroom now," she ordered.

"Is everything okay?" Dakota's husband, Bishop asked.

"Yes, fine." She jerked her head towards the restrooms and narrowed her eyes.

"We better go now." Dakota handed her drink to Bishop and pulled Asa along.

"You too, Pam," Asa yelled over her shoulder.

As soon as the four of them were inside, Melissa locked the door.

"What's going on?" Asa asked. "You look like something just scared the color out of you."

"I don't know. I feel like I'm having a panic attack, but I've never had one before, so I don't know." She dropped on the bench in the lounge just outside the stalls.

"Did something happen?" Dakota sat beside her and rubbed her arm.

The alarm in the three pairs of eyes staring didn't help. Pam fisted her fingers.

"I can't explain it. I was fine when I left home. I'm excited for Darius. He deserves this party, but I feel like we're being dishonest. People are congratulating us and giving us antidotes about marriage and babies like everything is normal. His mother swears she can see our love. His father is making plans for Darius and me to spend the weekend at his place once the baby gets here." She stopped for a deep breath.

"From the way the two of you are smiling and touching, I thought you two had settled your differences too," Asa said. "I don't think his parents meant any harm."

"But don't you see? I was just beginning to find myself again. The gallery just opened. I have a condo that I adore. I'm making new friends. I'm living a life that I like, not one Darius forced me to accept. And now, everything is spinning out of control. I'm pregnant and Darius is living in the apartment. I feel like someone else is mapping my life again." She took a deep breath.

"What are you saying?" Dakota's eyes widened. "Are you wishing you weren't pregnant?"

"Oh, no. Not at all. The baby is the best part of all of this." She made a circle with her hands. "But, with the baby comes a whole lot of other stuff, and I'm not sure I want to sign on for the extras. Suppose Darius wants to move back to San Francisco or has some crazy notion that I should close up the gallery? I was finally in control of my own life, and now I feel like my control is slipping away."

"It doesn't have to," Dakota said. "We come from tough stock, Melissa. If you're happy with your life now, fight for it."

"Melissa, can't you tell by the way Darius is focused on you that his feelings for you are genuine? If I could find a man willing to do half the stuff he's done for you in the past few months, I'd stick to him like glue." Pam knelt in front of her and placed her hands on Melissa's knees. "Maybe your hormones have interfered with your intuition."

Melissa shook her head with such force her vision blurred. "No. I can't assume he's doing all this stuff for me. We're both committed to making sure the baby is loved and nurtured in a positive environment. And I know I'm willing to do anything to make sure we live up to our commitment. But, for me to interpret our actions as anything more would be crazy. Foolish. How could I have been so foolish again?"

Dakota squeezed her arm. "Miss. Tough-As-Nails, I think you and Darius need to have a real conversation. Mim always told us you can't hide from the truth, and I think for months you've done exactly that."

"What if my truth doesn't match his reality?" She fought back the emotion.

"Then you'll just have to accept the outcome, but at least you'll be making a decision with all the facts," Dakota said in a soft whisper.

Chapter Thirty-Nine

The ride home was quiet, giving Melissa too much time to rehash the evening in her head. Her thought processes were faulty for sure. Sleeping with Darius was proof. At first, she thought she was only satisfying her sexual desire, but she was pleasuring her heart too.

She'd spent days wondering why Pam took so long to get over Steve. Now, she understood the strength of love. In the dark interior of the limousine, she smirked at her stupidity. Thinking she was in control had been her folly.

"Did you enjoy the party?" Darius slid to her side of the car.

"Yes. I think everyone had a good time."

"Dan wanted to discuss my next tour, but I told him any more touring would have to wait until after the baby gets here."

"Do you think delaying is a good idea? You know, strike while the irons are hot and all."

He didn't reply for a moment. The silence hanging between them was a comfortable one. Instead of the worry that would have dogged her in the past, she believed in him.

"No, I'm not worried about being forgotten. I've accomplished so much. I'm not greedy."

"Wanting a career isn't asking too much." She wanted to give him a way out. If she could ease him into telling her what he really wanted, maybe then she'd have the courage to do the same.

"We have plenty of time to talk about our careers. Being stationary has given me time to relax and write music. I'm more fit and rested. Running around and touring takes a toll on the body."

Melissa closed her eyes. Her sisters were right. She couldn't delay the inevitable any longer. There was too much at stake now.

As soon as they walked into the apartment, Turbo greeted them.

"I'll walk the dog and be right back," Darius said as he attached the leash.

She nodded. The thick feeling in her throat grew bigger. As tough as she thought she was, she wasn't ready to change the shade of her life. The apartment was home because signs of Darius were everywhere. His records, his iPod, even his sheet music. If everything disappeared, what would be left?

She pushed open the door to the nursery. Just seeing the baby furniture doused her with reality. With her hand planted on her stomach, she let her eyes drift around the room. There was still a lot to do before she could call the decorating complete, but no matter what, she couldn't keep hiding from the inevitable.

****

Darius walked the dog the two blocks to the park before he allowed him to stop and sniff. He was wound as tight as Turbo and every step helped him release some of the excitement from the evening.

The night was a success. His parents had managed to be in the same place without casting a chill over the whole room. The two of them must have finally found what they needed from life. But his mother's words were like a bad note in his ears. He'd felt Melissa stiffen after her comment. As much as he wanted those words to be true, he had doubts. Playing house with Melissa was fun. He was ready to make it permanent again, but she seemed skittish. She needed more time to be coaxed into the idea.

He circled the park, allowing the dog to stop every few feet. No matter how long he delayed going home, sooner or later, he needed to tell her what was in his heart. The divorce papers were a constant reminder they had unfinished business. By now he thought she'd have forgiven him and destroyed the documents, but they remained on the table like a bomb about to explode.

After growing up with parents disconnected from each other, he couldn't do that to his son. If she can't forgive him, then they need to make some other permanent arrangements. He straightened his shoulders and tugged on the leash.

"Come on, Turbo; it's time to face the music. Even if they're playing a tune we don't want to hear."

Melissa wasn't in the living room when he returned. Happy to have a few more moments before talking with her, he removed the leash from the dog and strolled into the kitchen.

After popping the cap on the Corona, he sat on the bar stool and focused on the refrigerator. Even without asking her the question, he could sense her reply. If only he could script what he needed from her.

Three gulps and he emptied the bottle. After turning off the lights, he slipped into the bedroom. Melissa was curled around a pillow. Her breathing was steady and even. He stripped off his clothes and stepped over Turbo to climb into bed.

Like all the nights since the baby began kicking, he settled in behind her and placed his hand on her stomach. Her hair was damp and smelled like flowers. Careful not to wake her, he tried to slow his breathing. He'd been granted one more day. Maybe the magic he needed would come to him in his sleep.

Chapter Forty

Darius turned over in the empty bed without opening his eyes. He'd heard her get up over an hour ago. Stalling never solved anything and time wasn't for sale. He swung his legs over the edge of the bed and buried his face in his hands.

"There you are. I was beginning to wonder if you were ever going to wake up."

"Why are you up so early; it's only seven?"

"I've got to get some stuff done at the gallery. With only two more weeks left, I want to make sure Henri and Amanda can take care of everything while I'm away."

She'd changed into the shortest shirt ever made. The top half of her stomach was covered and the round smooth skin on the underside gleamed like sun on water. Her panties covered the small patch between her legs. "You make pregnant look so sexy, I'd like to keep you that way."

She put her hand on her hip and pushed out her round tush. "I may make this look easy, but believe me, it's not. My body will need a few years to recoup after this."

He pulled her down on top of him and ran his hands inside her panties. She squealed as he grabbed her firm butt cheeks and squeezed. "I can't get enough of you."

"And I thought I was the only one affected by my pregnancy. I see you kinda like all this extra stuff, don't you?"

"Melissa, I like everything about you. It may have taken me more time than it should have to realize how much you mean to me, but now, I know I want to fight for us."

She grew still and rolled off him onto the mattress. For several moments, neither of them said anything. The only sound was Turbo licking his big, hairy paw.

"I know we need to have this conversation. I've been thinking about us too."

"My mom's comment last night upset you, didn't it? I saw you coming out of the bathroom with your sisters and Pam. You were upset," he said while still lying on his back.

"Not by her comment. But, we've been playing house. The last few months have been so nice, I just pretended this was real. I don't know what to believe. I don't know if I can tell reality from make-believe."

"Why can't what we're doing be our real life now? If we both want this life, then what's stopping us from living it?"

She pulled on her bottom lip with her teeth before scrambling off the bed and beyond his reach. "I got to get going. My meeting…" She ran into the bathroom and closed the door.

He opened the door just as she turned on the shower and stepped into the stall. "Darius, I really don't have time for this conversation this morning. Can't we talk when I get home tonight? And put on some clothes." She turned her back to him.

"I'm not going away, Melissa. I'll be here when you get home. I'll be here tomorrow morning and the morning after that." He stood just outside the shower with his hands on the top of the door.

"Please don't come in here, Darius."

He opened the door and stepped in behind her. She dropped the soap at his feet. Either she was crying or water from the shower ran down her face.

"We need to talk," he said.

"I know. I'm just not ready," she pleaded with him.

"Ready for what? I'm not asking you to do anything. Just love me and let me love you."

"We've been trying for five years. Nothing is different now except you knocked me up."

"I'm different. Can't you tell?"

"Yeah, but for how long? Until the next phone call from Dan, or the next tour, or awards show, or the next something." Her voice grew louder with each accusation, and he deserved each one. But, he couldn't apologize again.

"You just have to trust me. Believe when I tell you this time, I'll be different."

Water splashed over them. Steam clouded the clear glass. She stood perfectly still, her arms clamped to her sides.

A stream of water trailed over her shoulder and over her breast. Her nipple hardened, but she didn't move. Her eyes never left his face.

"If my word isn't enough, I don't know what else I can give you." He held her tight as she released the sob she must have been holding back.

Chapter Forty-One

Melissa sat with her back to the door. Getting through the meeting with her staff was hard enough, but she couldn't hold back the tears a moment longer. Without smearing her mascara, she dabbed under her eyes and swiped her nose.

If only she could roll away all the hurt and unhappiness into one big ball and throw it out like trash, everything would be just fine.

Numbness hadn't gripped her like this since the night her parents were killed in the horrific accident that changed her life. Back then, she'd been too young to know the consequences of her actions. This time, whatever she decided wouldn't only impact her, but her child. Her shoulders sagged against the weight.

She snatched her purse from the drawer and marched out of her office. "Amanda, Henri, I'm leaving."

Amanda's eyes widened. "I thought you were here all day. What if—"

"You two can handle everything and you know how to reach me. Call me anytime if you need me. I really need to go." Without waiting for more protests, she walked out of the gallery.

She couldn't walk away from Darius. They had so much unfinished business. She had to give their marriage another try, and another one, if the first one didn't work. She owed herself, their baby, and him to try.

The moment she stuck her key in the lock of the front door, she prayed he was still there, still willing.

"Darius," she called to him and closed the door.

"In here, in the kitchen."

Her heart lifted, happy to hear his voice.

She found him on the stool in the kitchen. A half-empty Corona and the divorce documents were in front of him.

He held up the bottle. "I needed something a little harder than soda." He swallowed the last of the beer and set the bottle down. His eyes pierced her. "If this is what you want…"

"It's not what I want." She sounded so loud she hardly recognized her own voice. "We have an unfinished story. I want to know how it's going to end."

His face contorted. "What made you change your mind? You've only been gone a few hours, so what happened?"

She sat next to him. "Nothing happened. I know we've got some work to do, but I think we ought to try. I love you enough to keep trying until we get it right. Tell me you feel the same way."

He picked up the empty bottle and gazed inside the opening. His Adam's apple bobbed up and down. "See, here's the thing..."

"No, Darius, I just poured my heart out to you, don't tell me there's a thing. If you had a thing, why didn't you tell me this morning?"

"We've been married five years and you've filed for divorce twice. I don't want to live under the threat that you might get mad and file again. Melissa, you've got to commit. Really commit. Look at my dad. He thought he and mom were okay, and twenty years after he found out she was cheating and took her back, she still dumped him."

"I thought you wanted to try again. This morning you said--"

He reached for her hand. "I want to try. But either you're all in or we need to part ways now, while we can still tolerate each other."

She placed her hand on her hip. "And what are you going to do differently? I'm not the only one who needs to make some promises."

He tilted his chin like he was getting ready to take a blow. Despite the baby kicking, her stomach did an extra rumble. He slipped off the stool and dropped on one knee.

"Are you proposing?" Her eyes stung with tears.

"Shhh and no, I'm not asking you to marry me." He held her hand between his palms. "Melissa,

I promise, with all my heart and all that I am, to love you, cherish you and treat you like the jewel you are. I'll never again as long as I live, take you for granted. Every day, I'll put your happiness and joy before everything else. If you'll take care of my heart, I vow to take care of yours. Forever."

Her stomach made getting on the floor awkward, but she managed to get on one knee. "Yes, Darius. I'll take care of your heart, if you let me."

Chapter Forty-Two

Melissa settled into the armchair like a cow being lowered in front of a trough. Her stomach couldn't grow another inch; there was no more room in her. Every position she maneuvered her body into was only comfortable for a few minutes.

"Darius, am I as big as I feel?"

His eyes rolled over her and rested on her belly. "You're carrying my son. If you had to get ten times bigger, that would be fine. You've never been prettier to me." He bent to kiss her. His tongue lingered on her lips before finding her tongue.

"Let me play some music for you." Darius shuffled through his album collection. "Somewhere in here is the right music to coax the baby out of you."

"I'm a week late. I would have bet I was going to be early. I've never been late for anything." She pulled up her shirt and glared at her stomach. The skin was taut and hard.

"Instead of having someone else sing to me, why don't you sing for me?"

He helped her out of the chair. "I'll sing if you'll dance with me."

"You can't even hold me tight. I'm a mile away." She protested when he tried to pull her close.

"I can always find a way to hold on to you."
He pulled her closer

She dropped her head against his chest. "You've been so patient with me. And every day, I think I get crankier."

"You're fine. Now, son, come on out of there and give your mommy a break." He placed his mouth near her ear and started to sing.

Nothing feels as good as this
Never knew this kind of bliss
You're the life I dreamed
You're everything; you're everything
to me.

And all I'll ever need.

A sharp pain stopped her. She clutched her stomach.

"What's wrong?" Darius held her up just as another pain gripped her and buckled her knees.

"I think I just had a contraction. But it was too painful. If contractions are this painful, I can't take labor." She almost didn't feel the gush of water soaking her bare feet. Darius moved before she realized what was happening. He lifted her up and placed her on the kitchen stool.

"Baby, stay right there. I'll get your bag. Don't move." He reached in the closet and grabbed her bag. "I can carry you and the bag."

"Don't be silly. I can walk. I think walking will help with my labor. I know everybody says this, but you know when we come back, our lives won't be the same."

"It's going to be better. So much fuller."

****

Darius stood at the head of the bed next to her. Melissa was tough. Watching what she had to go through showed him she was strong. Unable to find the words to express what he felt, all he could do was brush away the hair plastered to her temple.

Her labor lasted too long. The pushing, the breathing, and the panting were endless. Two hours should have been enough, but she endured seven. Her resilience had no limits.

She managed a smile. Finally, the pain in her face had vanished, but she continued to cry.

"Honey, please stop crying," he whispered in her ear as he stroked her forehead.

"I can't help it, Darius. Every time I think I'm done, they start again." She shifted the baby in her arms and cooed to him. "He's beautiful, isn't he?"

"Yes. And I have something special for his mother." He lifted the baby out of her arms and placed him in the bassinet. Melissa glanced at him through her long, wet lashes. "This is for you." He placed the big box in her lap.

"What is this?" she asked as she tore the wrapping away from the big box.

He rocked the baby's bed without answering her. She pulled the box free and raised the lid.

"The boots." She gushed. "Darius, you bought them for me. How could you even remember what they looked like?"

"I should never have forgotten." He kissed her forehead.

"I love you so much," she whispered.

Not trusting his voice, he nodded. Coming so close to losing everything was hard to admit. Watching Melissa hold their son was better than anything he'd thought he wanted. In the sterile, white hospital room, his life was happier than he thought possible.

Epilogue

Melissa slipped into the gown Asa had made just for her. Her hips were a little fuller than they used to be, but her stomach was flat again. She examined herself in the three-way mirror of their suite and nodded.

A year ago, this life was unimaginable. In the last five months, she'd become a wife again and a mother. Hitting the lottery couldn't have brought her more joy. When she returned to Philly in a few days, she'd start decorating the house they'd purchased in Rittenhouse Square. Nothing from San Francisco had made the cut and only a few items from the condo. Tonight she could be Cinderella getting ready for the big ball. Since the day they both got down on their knees and committed to their marriage, neither had spoken a cruel word. The ones said during labor didn't count. Nothing during those hours could be held against her.

"Yeah, you look good, baby." She spun around to see Darius leaning against the door jamb holding DJ in one arm like a football.

"I didn't hear you come in." She sashayed toward him and kissed the baby's full head of black curls. "You clean up good in a tux, Mr. Bellamy."

"Not as good as you look in that dress. Girl, if you keep looking so sexy, you're going to be pregnant again in a hot minute."

"I was just thinking about how far we've come. The last time you went to the Academy Awards, I had to stay home. Remember?"

"I was stupid. If I could, I'd even take DJ with us tonight."

"Oh, no, this is our night. We haven't been away from him for more than a few hours since we brought him home. We've flown the best au pair in the country out here just so we could celebrate tonight. And we're going to do the night up right. My sisters are here, your parents are here, and our friends are here. You understand, don't you, DJ?"

A long trail of drool hung from the baby's mouth almost to the floor. Melissa reached for the drool cloth on Darius's shoulder and wiped his mouth.

"You're right. You deserve this night and I'm going to make sure it's special." He reached for her hand and twirled her around.

"If you keep this up, he's going to mess up your tux and you'll have to wear jeans."

He lifted the baby up until the tips of their noses touched. "I wouldn't even care. I used to think getting the Academy Award for best music score would be my crowning glory. Ha, was I wrong."

The baby started to coo and flashed a wet, toothless grin.

Claire appeared behind Darius. "It's time for me to feed him and put him down for the night."

"Good night, champ." Darius kissed DJ's forehead and handed him over to the au pair.

"Wait, I need to kiss him too. We might not get back to the hotel until tomorrow morning." She cradled him in her arms and cooed him until he quieted.

"Don't look so sad, Melissa. Didn't you just give me a big lecture about this being our night?" He eased the baby out of her arms and handed him over to Claire.

"You're right. Let me put on the six-inch heels I just had to have and let's go win your gold statue."

Other books in the series:
The Sweet Road to Home

A house brought them together, but will it tear their love apart?

Determined, Asa Conroy has moved back to Bristol to organize her life. The house where she grew up is just the place to take control of her future. But her happy return home is soon quashed when she finds out the house is slated for demolition by the same man that shunned her in high school.

Career-driven Simeon Harper is one construction project away from erasing his dysfunctional past and fulfilling his promises to his dying mother.

When these two childhood friends collide, will they be able to salvage their love, or does it go down in the rubble?

The Sweet Road to Love

Bookstore owner Dakota Conroy has been dumped by her long-distance boyfriend. While the sting is still branded in her brain, she decides to pour her excess energy into the store's renovation with the help of engineering specialist, Bishop Contee. His charm is irresistible, but his reputation for

womanizing is legendary. Could he be a nice
distraction while she mends her life?

Bishop Contee enjoys his women like he enjoys a
fine glass of wine. When it comes to sowing his
wild oats, he still has a pocketful. Besides, helping
his sister get her life together is enough
domestication for him. When he stumbles upon the
eclectic beauty of Dakota, he's caught with his
guard down.

Playing with fire is dangerous. Will these two take
the risk for a lifetime together?

JOIN THE JACKI KELLY NEWSLETTER at Jackikelly.com!

So you can stay tuned to new releases, appearance, and events and prizes. She's always giving something away.

ABOUT THE AUTHOR

Jacki Kelly has written dozens of short stories and several books. She lives in the North East with her husband and one loveable dog. She loves hearing from her readers so please contact her.

Connect with her online:
http://www.jackikelly.com
Twitter - @jackikellybooks
http://facebook.com/jackikellyauthor

If you enjoyed reading The Sweet Road Back, please tell everyone you know. Please post a review for other readers on your favorite reading forum.

Trademarks:

True Religion; True Religion Apparel, Inc.
Corvette; General Motors Company
Manolo Blahnik; Manolo Blahnik
Birkin; Hermès International S.A.
Friends; Warner Bros. Television
Corona; Grupo Modelo, Anheuser Busch InBev
iPod; Apple Inc.